One

Cita had finished the sweeping, the day Alphonse brought the white woman. Fetched the water and moved the pig, washed the clothes, spread them on the bush, away from the house. Fed the little ones three times over by the time Alphonse came along the path with the woman. Swept from the path to the house and under the house, not a leaf anywhere, just as she had today.

Along the path came Alphonse, giving his little whistle: hoo-hwee. Rafael had looked up: ah, my brother. Up the steps came that brother and behind him, the foreign woman. He whistled again at the curtain, drawing it aside and seeing Cita herself standing there with the baby on her hip. He's not here? he asked. Rafael stood up and came into the light. I am here, he said. She had looked over Alphonse's shoulder at the woman's face and seen what was written there.

She now rested the broom in the corner, picked up the baby and allowed it to suck. She rocked slowly, backwards and forwards, the picture moving through her mind from the beginning. She had finished the sweeping, the day Alphonse brought the white woman.

Alphonse could not resist it. Passing by Cita's place in the forest on their little tour, how could he resist? He must show his new friend everything, he had promised. Rafael hadn't been in the town for a few days; he was therefore at Cita's, playing father to his brood. It was uncomfortable to visit him there, naturally. Just a quick nod to say hello, and: this is Emma, from England.

Rafael had already seen Emma in the town but now he, Alphonse, could introduce her with a touch of propriety, for he, Alphonse, had slept with her.

Slept with her in a sense. Not exactly, no. He hadn't been aroused – rather, mystified by the idea of riding all that generous, pink flesh. Much of which he had touched. A fatted calf. He liked the juxtaposition of those English words with their echo of things biblical. Their sacrificial connotations weren't accurate, of course, but she was calf-like and wondrously fat. See, he mused to himself. I have landed the fatted calf. She came obediently behind him now along the path; they would cross the river and join the path at the top.

Emma felt more alive than she ever had in her life before. Though it was hot. By the middle of the day the insides of her brain were melting and a stream of sweat ran off her back where her rucksack pressed the shirt against her skin. She mopped her armpits surreptitiously. Alphonse turned back with a look of concern. He was being so marvellous.

Deep down she had always known that the world was like this. It was incredible to think of all those people in their offices in London, still living their grey lives, and here in the Philippines, on the other side of the world – this. Life, bursting out everywhere. Those great big red flowers. Those dangly pink ones. That heavenly smell. Kalasutsi? she ventured. Alphonse nodded. Yes, kalasutsi. You learn very quick. Filipina ikaw. You are a Filipina!

He was handsome: small and slight. They were all like that. Beside them the English seemed bumbling and oafish – herself included. She felt it keenly. Yet, thanks to the phenomenon of cultural exchange, Filipinos found her attractive too. In that house at the tea party a woman had sidled up to her shyly and touched her arm. Excuse, I have a baby, she had said, patting her tiny, curved stomach. I pray he have nose like you.

In my country, Emma said over and over again, I'm just ordinary. No, no, they replied, grinning over perfect white teeth. English very beautiful. Guapa. Guapa ikaw.

She gave a little cry of surprise; she wasn't paying attention. They had been following a river for a while, and now Alphonse had lightly stepped across, apparently on thin air. But no, above the swirling water was a yellow stick, not much thicker than a bamboo. On closer inspection she saw that it was a bamboo. The look of concern again shadowed his face and he danced back to take her hand. Now she, the clumsy foreign one who had been walking along Tottenham Court Road just two weeks before, must follow her guide.

The river was not very broad, nor did the water run fast, but it was exhilarating. She was Tintin, she was Jonny Quest, she was Roger and Hal from the adventure books. Somewhere under her white skin she had the balance of a native; she could cross ravines. Her father had always wanted a boy.

Cita sat on the swinging seat, fanning herself and the baby at her side. Her daughter slept in the shade beneath them; the boy was sprawled outside under the trees, the old woman inside, on the bed. Heat hung heavy and the flies buzzed slowly in the afternoon.

It had been like a pebble thrown into water, when the white woman came. She had climbed the ladder – Cita opened her eyes a little and studied the wooden steps, saw how the soft fat feet in their sandals had climbed them, one, two, three, four. This was an old trick, taught to her by her grandmother, this power of memory, squeezed open by imagination, following a moment like a pebble all the way down into the dark water of the past. Even in dark water she could follow it, keep track of it, feel where it lay on the river bed. And all the while ripples fanned out on the surface, which was the future.

She saw the soft fat feet on the steps of the ladder. Sores on those ankles, the bites of mosquitoes. Big thighs, without grip. Shorts and a shirt like a man, a bag, pink shoulders and hair yellow-brown, the colour of a dead toad. Cita sat, quietly moving the fan. I can see you, white woman. I have you in my inner eye. Your skin is spotted with brown freckles like Father O'Hara's. Covered, like his, with tiny yellow hairs.

Now Alphonse suggested cooling off in the river and there they sat, in the shallows, giggling like children. It was remarkably easy. Emma reached out and touched his hair. I can't believe how black it is, she said. The water makes it even blacker. He laughed and moved his head. Funny Emma. Nice Emma. Her clothes stuck to her. She turned her shoulders away from him to hide her breasts but there they were, no matter how she tweaked at her shirt as they climbed out.

Cool now, yes? Yes. She smiled and the shirt stuck to her. All he needed to do was to show her things and tell her their names in Visayan. A nice girl. His friend, Emma.

By the time they reached the path they were dry again, and hungry. Alphonse apologised. I am sorry we could not eat with Rafael at the hut. He wagged his head. It is bad for him. Emma shielded her eyes with her hand against the glare of the road, and the whitened earth blazed back. Bad for him? How do you mean? Is that his wife? Alphonse spat. No. She is a servant. She was a servant in our family house. He cannot marry a servant. But they have children? she asked. Yes. They have children.

They came to a little stall and stepped up to the tiny platform. In its cave the usual things stood on shelves. This, sari-sari store. It mean: everything. Soap, candles, matches, sweets. Under a net, something wrapped in leaves. Bud-bud, he said. Rice and coconut. Good. We buy. Can I do it? asked Emma. Let me try. Two, please, she pointed. Salamaat. Alphonse took a cigarette from a jar, crossing his index fingers to indicate that they could share it, half each. English women smoked; American also. Alcohol, also. He lighted it where the flames flickered in a well of paraffin. Come, Emma. Filipina-ka.

The road shimmered. In the forest, swinging in the shade with her eyes closed, Cita watched them go.

'Why was I told that these people can be hostile? That I'd feel threatened?'

'Who said that? It wasn't field office.'

'That German guy in Manila.'

'Dieter? He's been here too long.'

'Mm.'

Emma sat on Valerie's patio. Val had her hammock out there; she was marking papers. There were children gathered in a knot on the path again, peering in through the open concrete blocks of the wall.

'Why do they always do that?'

'You get used to it.'

'What's so interesting?'

'You are. We are. You find *them* interesting, don't you?'

'Yes, but I don't stare.'

'They do.'

Emma went into the kitchen. A lizard on the wall lifted its head, froze for a moment and scuttled behind the fridge. The fridge hummed and creaked. She opened the door and gingerly extracted a bottle of water. The tin cans gave electric shocks: something to do with the appliances not being earthed properly.

'Water?'

'Thanks.'

'I'd kill for a cold Coke.'

'You know where they sell it.'

'Oh God, I couldn't walk to Rico's in this heat.'

'Take a pedicab.'

'I couldn't even walk to the road.'

'Well, take a shower. Look, I've got to get on with this. You want some advice? Leave out the Coke. All that sugar just makes you hotter. Stick to water.'

Emma wandered into her room and lay down on the pallet that was her bed. It was too hot to move. Then she heaved herself up and draped a towel over her feet. The bites were suppurating. Instead of drying and healing, the edges stayed open, full of yellow stuff. The flies wouldn't leave them alone. She'd just had a letter from her mother which warned her about mosquito bites going gangrenous in the tropics. It was awful sometimes. She had the wrong body; she was covered with the wrong skin.

An insect buzzing at the window awoke her, hours later. It was miraculously cooler; she could breathe again. Voices floated up from downstairs in the space between the walls and ceiling. '...a teeny bit self-indulgent...' came Charles' voice, fading out towards the patio.

She showered under the pipe, letting the tepid water flow. A dusting of baby powder, a loose dress, and she was ready to be sociable.

'Ah! And how's our young adventuress this afternoon?'

'Fine. Anyone seen my ciggies?'

'Here.' Charles tossed a packet across to her.

'These are like smoking toothpaste.'

'Cheap, though. Those imports of yours cost a fortune. We're thinking of going to the beach hut tonight with the faculty. Want to come?'

'For the night?'

'Yup. Sleeping under the stars. Field trip, sort of thing.'

'What do I need to bring?'

'Nothing. Wala. Just your sense of the aesthetic.'

As Charles' old truck rattled away from the town along a dirt track through the villages, Emma gazed out at the huts and trees and her spirits rose. There was a path through the palms. Where those palms met the sand, a tiny hut on stilts.

Charles dumped his bag and waded straight into the water in his shorts.

'Coming in? You're all right here. It's sandy. Might be a few jellyfish.'

Emma sat on a log. The mosquito bites hurt; she didn't want to get sand in them. She applied a bit more antiseptic cream.

'Shift yourself, lazy. There's wood to collect.'

'Oh.'

The students were dragging old palm leaves and branches into a pile, Valerie showing them something, as if she knew best. It was the wrong attitude, Emma thought. We come from our world and say: this is how to live, this is how to do it. How do we know any better than they do?

The sky turned scarlet and orange, the sun dropped down quickly. A few little boats skimmed over the flat pink sheet of the sea.

'Siloy! Measure the rice, will you? How many are we? Nine? Alphonse said he might come. Come on, do the eggs, will you?'

Emma just wanted to sit. To drink it all in, to be open to everything, open, open, open. There was Charles, cross-legged and gazing out to sea, a picture of a white man lording it over the colonies. She moved forward, next to Valerie.

'What's that island called, out there? The big one?'

'Siquijor.'

'Does that mean anything?'

'Don't think so. Might do.'

'Is Rafael coming with Alphonse, did he say?'

'Expect so. Why?' Valerie poked her in the ribs. 'You've not taken a fancy to Rafael, by any chance?'

'Of course not.'

'Well! No accounting for taste. I thought you'd taken a shine to Alphonse.'

'Don't be daft. It's not like that. He probably wouldn't be interested anyway.'

'Rafael? You bet he would. You're foreign, aren't you? He'd be interested all right. Go carefully.'

'What d'you mean?'

'Nothing. Enjoy yourself. That's what we're here for, aren't we?'

'I thought you were here to teach social sciences.'

'I mean on this earth, dingbat. We're here on this earth to enjoy ourselves, aren't we?'

Alphonse rapped sharply against the side of the bus with a peso and the boy yelled to the driver to stop. It was about here that the students had their hut and the professors planned to picnic tonight. It might turn out to be a party, it might not.

He had learned a great deal at the last party. Not in the same vein as his own family gatherings; there had been less food and more beer, for one thing. The casual references to things cosmopolitan had fired his imagination – very Hemingway, very Scott Fitzgerald. Alphonse was passionately fond of literature – the classics, and, of course, poetry.

He had his poetry book always with him in his red

shoulder bag. *The Penguin Book of English Poetry*, a seventh edition. Emma knew many of the poems and this forged a link across the great divide. He knew them all, and some of the shorter ones by heart. He murmured now as he went softly through the dark trees. *Sunset and evening star, and one clear call for me, and may there be no moaning of the bar, when I put out to sea, but such a tide as moving seems asleep, too full for sound and foam...*

He couldn't retrieve the next line, though it was in his head somewhere. Anyway, he could see the glow of a fire; he was almost there.

Emma saw him step out of the dusk and watched him approach with an eager face. He squeezed down beside her on the log, beaming. No, no, Rafael had not come, he was attending to a little business. He, Alphonse, had come alone. Alone, but in the company of the great masters. He patted his bag and extracted the book. Between the worn pages there nestled two thin reefers. The great masters and also, he added roguishly, a little *kuan*.

This gathering of the English people was not the same as the last. Emma objected to the sight of a fish split open over the coals and the debate took on a more contentious edge. She didn't eat fish. She didn't eat anything of a savoury nature, as far as Alphonse could make out, but a bland diet of plants. This was reflected in her bland body and perhaps the sweetish smell that clung to it. She was vegetarian.

Charles, brown and lithe as a Filipino, though startlingly

white at the edge of his shorts, spoke to her sternly. When in Rome, he said. This was not an easy phrase for Alphonse; probably something was lost in the translation. He did not think in English. Some foreign concepts did not stand up to the mental transfer. Emma vehemently declared that she would not sacrifice something. Alphonse excused himself, moved around the back of the fire and squatted down beside Charles. They could have a little smoke, perhaps? Later.

They lay back on the sand, staring up into the stars. A distance away, the students were settling down into their blankets with a few muffled shrieks of laughter. Alphonse and Charles were quietly and amicably out of their heads.

'See that yellow star over there?'

'O-o. I see it.'

'No, not that one. Over there.'

'Behind the red one, no?'

'What red one?'

'You don't see the red one?'

'Nope. My God, it's amazing.'

'Amazing.'

'I'm falling backwards. Are you?'

'O-o. Backwards.'

'And forwards.'

'O-o.'

There was a pause, then Alphonse added, '*When that which drew from out the boundless deep, turns again for home.*'

'You what?'

'Alfred, Lord Tennyson. No?'

'You're an old humbug, Alphonse.'

'What is humbug?'

'It's... like lying here looking at all that and not under-standing a damn thing about anything.'

Emma lay in the doorway of the hut. There was only room for two stretched out inside and Valerie was already asleep beside her. What a night. What a sky. Little tongues of lightning flashed on the horizon, far out to sea. This was the real world. She would live here always, and have a husband, and let her blood mix and be thickened by generations of Filipino blood, her children and grand-children – with big dark eyes – playing on the beach under a great hot sky.

Two

Cita swept under the house and around the bottom of the steps. She stooped over the hand broom, one arm across her supple back, flicking the leaves aside this way and that, swish, swish, along the path as far as the banana trees. It was a green, humid morning. Today surely he would come.

Boy-boy had run off to the fish-traps at dawn. She would keep Juanita with her, no disappearing into the bush. There were eggs to take down to the store and paraffin to collect. She shooed the chickens from under her feet and placed three more eggs with care into the corner of her skirt. The pig, tethered beneath the kitchen, shambled to its feet as she passed.

On the balcony she put the eggs into the basket with those from yesterday.

'Nita! Nita!'

The girl lifted the curtain. Cita scolded her to hurry, bring the clothes. She wasn't big enough yet to carry the tub but she could bring the soap and brush. The old woman could take the eggs. Cita swung the baby onto her back, knotted the cloth over her chest and lifted the tub up to her head. She set off with Juanita for the river.

When they came home later, her grandmother had not taken the eggs. It didn't matter, said the old lady; they would keep for tomorrow. She had been picking kala-mungi. We need paraffin, said Cita. We have candles, said her grandmother, plucking off the leaves. No, Cita insisted. Today we need paraffin. Perhaps Rafael will come.

The baby was fed. He slept on her back. She thrust a green mango at the girl and took the basket on her hip. It was a long walk down to the road.

Charles had left Dumaguete with his students a few days before, heading for a volcano in the north of the island – a dormant volcano but believed to be inhabited by spirits. Emma watched their makeshift expedition depart with mixed feelings. They all seemed to know what they were looking for.

She herself had no clear reasons for being there. She told everyone that she was a writer, but this was untrue. She sat at Valerie's desk with paper in front of her and a pen in her hand, and nothing would come.

She was weighed down by the house. It was the only concrete construction on the outskirts of the town and it sat heavily over her, brooding and ugly. The tiny wood and nipa huts between the trees were delicate, light; they breathed. The concrete house harboured life of its own, certainly – spiders, mice, frogs, ants, lizards, flies, mosquitoes.

A flash of colour caught her eye. Those damned kids again, taking the fruit – what were those little oranges called? Kalamansi. Yes, they were taking the kalamansi off the tree that stood inside the wall. Honestly. They were hers – hers and Valerie's and Charles'. They rented the place, didn't they?

Emma hurried out. 'No!' she cried. 'Stop that! No take kalamansi! Bad!' One snot-nosed urchin reached out for another, grinning broadly. Emma slapped his outstretched arm, hard. With whoops of laughter they fled into the bushes.

She was hot all over. Her hand stung. She had wanted to pick the little oranges herself to make juice, to put some in the fridge for the others – her contribution. She looked at her hand in disgust. She'd hurt a child. Though he hadn't seemed hurt. He'd just laughed.

She blew her nose on some loo paper. It was wrong to waste loo paper; it was expensive. It was uselessly thin, anyway. Everything was useless. The sweat ran down from under her bra. It was the house, the semi-westernised house that was getting to her. It held her back, it stood between her and Out There.

She had to get back to basics. Otherwise it made no sense to be in the Far East at all. She would go and spend a couple of nights at the beach hut, alone.

The bus stood at the edge of the market in the dust. Its name, 'Our Lady', was painted in red and green letters above the space where the driver's window might have been. There were no windowpanes. Emma approached uncertainly.

Zamboanguita. Valerie had said that it was the Zamboanguita bus and that she would have to recognise the right place to get off, after two barrios and then a kilometre or so along the road. I'll recognise it, Emma had assured her. I've got a photographic memory. I take in a lot of detail from my surroundings.

She climbed in, into the welcome shade. The heat was stupefying, even so. Two young girls followed and sat down with shy smiling glances in her direction. Emma noticed that their slim arms hardly touched the material of their lacy dresses, leaving room for air to circulate. Her own shirt clung to her all over, though cotton was supposed to be cool. Maybe it was the wrong sort of cotton.

The bus filled with people. She ought to have checked that this was, indeed, the right bus; she could be heading in the wrong direction. The girls, who were probably students and might speak some English, were now hidden behind a man who had a chicken pinned beneath each arm. Another boarded with two small goats. The seat next to Emma was the last to be taken, empty until an elderly woman squeezed in with several bags and a bucket filled to the brim with something liquid and green.

The loaded bus, filled with voices and squawking, sat

motionless in the sun. At last a young man with a red bandana tied over his head emerged from a nearby store, wiped his mouth, and climbed into the driver's seat through the window.

Emma sat rigid. The bus rumbled into life, the liquid in the pail slopped from rim to rim. It looked like overcooked spinach, or seaweed. She held her bag tightly. Grit flew through the window into her eyes. They stopped somewhere. Was this the first barrio? She wasn't concentrating. People piled out with baskets, sacks, chickens. More piled in. She stared out anxiously. She must remember where to get off.

It was here. 'Here!' she cried. 'Stop. Please!' Someone banged on the roof, the bus screeched to halt. A youth at the door was waiting for her fare and she raised her hands in question. How much? He said something. Sorry? Pifty. Pifty centavo.

She stood alone at the side of a road that vanished into trees in both directions. But this was the place, she was sure. Charles had left the truck just there, last week. She had an infallible sense of these things. It was instinct.

She set off through the palms. Each one had a metal band nailed around the bole; she knew about this – it was to stop rats climbing up for the coconuts. Odd that the bands were nailed at such varying heights; some at twenty feet or more. Kalubihan, a group of such palms. She would make a list of all the words she knew so far. She would fill her hours of solitude slowly, and well. She wouldn't actually measure them at all; she would lose track of time.

The path didn't lead her to exactly the same spot but she wasn't far off. She came to the beach within sight of some huts and boats to the left: therefore the beach hut she sought must be further round to the right. It was. Thankfully she mounted the rickety steps and dropped her bag in the corner. She'd made it.

Well, then. Where did one begin? There was no beginning, middle or end. She looked about. The hut needed repairs; there were holes in the thatch. It looked like a simple enough job.

There were long palm fronds to be found on the sand nearby. The edges cut her hands until she thought of using her penknife. After a few minutes of weaving them in and out of the roof, she turned around. She was being watched. A group of children, their hair stiff and tawny from seawater, stared at her. They might have been the same children as those in the town, with the same black, slanting eyes. Emma smiled briefly. She stopped her weaving and ducked into the hut, leaning back against the creaking wall with a sigh of annoyance.

After a while she looked out. The group had crept closer. The bigger children had babies on their hips. They might have been young women; it was hard to tell.

'What ees the time?'

'I'm sorry, I don't know.'

They grinned and nodded.

'What ees the time? What ees your name?'

'Emma. Em-ma.'

They shrieked with laughter. Em-ma. Em-ma. They showed no sign of leaving whatsoever, but sat down, managing to edge nearer at the same time. Oranis Caballeros, announced a boy, pointing to his chest. Nina Caballeros, my seester. My brother. My cousin. Yes, yes.

Emma fetched her journal and pen. She pointed to herself. 'Magsusulat.' According to Alphonse this meant: writer. If they saw that she was a writer perhaps they would move away. She began her list of words. Salamaat, thank you. O-o, yes. Tubig, water. Barrio, village. Kapoy, tired. Gabii, night. Buntag, morning. Lamok, mosquito. She looked up. They were watching her intently, craning their necks. Pero, but. Bulan, moon. Saging, banana. Bo-ongon, grapefruit. Itlog, egg.

It was no good. She wanted to swim, but it would be quite impossible in front of such an audience. Filipinas never swam in bathing costumes, but in their dresses.

'Okay. Sleep now. Er... tulog. Bye-bye.' She closed the book with a clap, waved and smiled and moved out of sight, into the hut. It was dim and smelled like the inside of a tent. Dampness and air and salt and earth. She unpacked the contents of her bag. She had some bananas, mangos, water – no cigarettes, for this was to be a cleansing time, body and soul. There was also her torch, penknife, shirt, towel, swimsuit, shawl and antiseptic cream. A minimum of possessions, though it seemed a lot. She wrapped herself in the shawl and lay down across the ridges of bamboo, prepared for a long vigil, longer at least than that of the watchers outside.

She could have brought her book. She was reading Sartre. Perhaps, after all, it would not have been appropriate.

The flatlands were drained of their colour and fell into shadow long before the hilltops lost the sun. It became dark in the forest. The old lady took her time picking over the rice. Her hands moved over the flat basket with terrible patience, flicking out the grit.

Cita pushed another husk under the flames. She had ground the coconut and used the milk; it bubbled now in the pot with the purple heart of the banana. She twirled a twig between her hands in the mixture, lifting out the fibres. Some lemon grass. Good. Another husk under the flames.

The pig snuffled below the lattice of the floor. Juanita rocked the baby. Boy would bring the fish home soon, and Rafael would surely come when it was dark.

The light gradually lost its brilliance. Emma peeked cautiously through a gap in the slats. An empty beach. She changed into her swimsuit and stepped out across the sand. The air was warm on her skin and the sea lay at her feet. She wiggled her toes in the shallows with delight, scooping handfuls over her shoulders, down her back. She sank under its silky surface. It was divine, a spiritual experience. But the low angle of the sun made it rather difficult to see the bottom; she didn't like to swim out too far. Best to be sensible.

Afterwards she ate a mango and two bananas. They were small bananas and a curious pinky red. She was starving hungry and ate two more. The sand itched her bites, which had just begun to get better at last. But she was not there for her physical needs. The sky flared up in bright Technicolor and between the islands, on the far edge of the sky – edge of the world, maybe – there was a frill of lightning.

Then it was dark. She squatted a little way off for a wee before climbing back, then stuffed some things into her bag to make a pillow, settling near the doorway as she had the week before, and looking out at the stars. The strange, rich stars. They made her feel excited, and daring, and happy. If she had invited Alphonse to join her out here, he would have come, and she regretted it for a moment. But it was better not to complicate things. It was all platonic between them now.

She was jerked out of sleep by a man's voice.

'Hey.'

Her eyes were open but she didn't move. Blackness. Silence. Then again, from the other side of the hut, low and unhurried.

'Hey.'

She had rolled away from the doorway in her sleep but

her eyes were fixed on the opening, which hung like a square of embroidery in the dark. Then the pinpoints of light were obliterated, and reappeared, as a man's figure moved across. Then the voice came from behind the hut, inches from her head.

'Hey.'

Her jaw was clenched; fear banged under her ribs. Then something, someone, jumped up at the bamboo frame and shook it hard. Pieces of twig and leaf showered down. Then silence again. The seconds ticked by.

'I rape you.'

She was going to die. It suddenly seemed quite possible, quite likely. Her hand touched the torch and slowly, quietly, felt for the knife. She opened the blade.

With a great rustling and swishing, the hut shook again.

'Hey I rape you.'

She was out on the sand, flashing the torch wildly in all directions, flashing the knife, shouting at the top of her voice GET AWAY FROM ME YOU STUPID STUPID BASTARD – nonsense, nonsense, she didn't know what came out of her mouth so deep and harshly, driven by terror. She ran through the trees, suddenly nimble as a goat, shouting, shouting, swinging the torch.

She reached the road. No one followed, she had seen no one. The lights of a truck came into view, heading for Dumaguete. She waved her arms and it came to a stop. Climbing up into the cab and seeing the eyes and teeth of the driver gleaming in the dark, she knew a moment of doubt. But there was no choice. They roared off into the night, the headlights picking out strange devilish shapes in the undergrowth. She trembled violently. He spoke, not in English. He pointed back along the road, and drew a finger across his throat.

At the crossroads in the town he brought the truck to a shuddering halt. She was free to go. He had understood that the mad white woman by the road in the middle of nowhere had needed to come to the town. Salamaat, she said fervently. Free to go.

She knew it could not yet be midnight. There was for some reason a midnight curfew and all the streets would be empty, but along the Main Street she could hear the thump of music from the place they called the Red Rooster. She hesitated and then turned down a side street. She didn't dare to venture past the nightclub, though Valerie and Charles had been there. It was just a shack, they said. It was also a brothel.

She could go to Alphonse and Rafael's place – it was just down there. But she was afraid of everything. They were gentle, they were hostile; she was a visitor, she was a whore. The buffaloes pulled the carts; the international jets flew through the sky.

A pot crashed to the ground, sending the hens scattering into the bush. The little girl froze. It was morning; her father had just arrived and drawn the curtain aside and was silhouetted against the bright sun. Crash. Crash. No! he said, catching her mother's wrist. What are you doing?

Oh, cried her mother, I can smell her on you. What nonsense are you talking? he asked. Oh, I can smell that white woman as large and foul as a durian.

Juanita felt his anger. He stopped to pick up the food but it had dribbled through the slats. The pig grunted happily. Her father grabbed her mother again and said you must not waste food it is a sin but her mother screamed you have been to the house of the white people I know you have, and meanwhile her grandmother sat in the corner, covering her eyes.

Then he turned and climbed back down the steps while her mother screamed after him: I know what you do, I know how you make your money; I will tell Loloy. Uncle Loloy was a policeman. Her father was gone and mother stood there, pulling her hair.

Emma lay on the pallet, looking at the sun pushing through the shutters that they called jalousies. Nobody had heard her come back in the middle of the night. She'd never tell anyone what happened, what had nearly happened. Never.

She looked across the room. The burned mosquito coil had a small pile of grey ash beneath it. The floorboards held her heap of possessions in the corner. The paperback at her side bore the title *The Age of Reason*. She scratched at the new bites on her arms. She was alive. She was unscathed.

Wrapped in a sheet, she went downstairs. Charles and Valerie had already left but there were signs of company from the previous night – empty beer bottles, some with candles stuck into them and wax dribbled down the sides; full ashtrays, cassettes all over the floor. Emma tidied these as best she could and stacked them in the fridge. Charles had said that heat made them warp. There was no milk. She longed suddenly for breakfast – not bananas but real breakfast, muesli and cold milk. Bread.

She pulled on shorts and a shirt and went out. The world had to be faced, and the sooner the better before the heat slammed down and nailed her to the shade. A few children scampered across the path, calling to one another. They were not interested in her really; even so, she felt the eyes of judgement upon her as though she had transgressed, or exposed herself indecently in a public place.

A bridge crossed the culvert where the path met the town road. Women walked along in their shifts of bright colours, baskets on hips and on their heads. They nodded and smiled, speaking a few trilling sentences as Emma passed them with her London stride. She smiled back, vast as an elephant. The hot air sat on her shoulders and wrapped itself around her neck.

A pedicab raced by, a scooter with a little sidecar. She could hail it and take a ride, but she was unsure about speaking to the driver and how much to pay him. She walked on.

The welcome smell of baking met her outside Rico's. The Filipinos didn't seem to eat bread; it was baked mostly for foreigners, for visitors, for a novelty. The tiny diamond-shaped rolls were swollen and yeasty. She bought a dozen and then browsed along the shelves, picking up this and that, the merchandise of home. Dusty tins of coffee, apparently untouched for years, tins of pineapple, tubes of toothpaste. She studied a box of tea bags: Black Cat tea bags, made in China. Her own box brought from England, bought at the corner shop at the end of Sutton Terrace on that free-falling day before the flight, was almost finished. She paused at the Johnson's baby powder. She still had some left, which she was trying to eke out.

She bought three more rolls with a coconut drink and secured a table in the café. The table secured her: the whole of Rico's was a womb protecting her from the torrid, teeming nightmare outside. But it wasn't a nightmare. She must get a grip on herself. She dispatched the rolls quickly, pushing the sweet, chewy dough into her mouth. The drink was also white and glutinous. A fan in the corner whirred and shook.

An odd, clammy feeling went through her, as if she might be unwell. There were all sorts of fevers you could get in the tropics. She glanced up. That woman outside, with the baby – she knew that face. Surely it was Rafael's... what was her name? That woman Alphonse had called a servant. Why was she staring like that?

Emma dropped her eyes. The giddy feeling rose and fell; it must be the sudden sugar intake. In this climate you couldn't get away with it. She'd be okay in a minute.

When she looked up, the woman and child were no

longer there. Funny that she'd seen them, just when she'd been thinking about Rafael. She thought about him quite a lot. He was... well, she didn't know yet, but she looked forward to seeing him again. She hadn't seen either of the brothers for a while, but that was how it was in the Far East. You couldn't expect anything; you couldn't pin things down. You had to have an open mind about everything.

Three

Hidden behind a line of washing in the yard, Alphonse lay with his eyes closed and his hands behind his head. There was no hurry. Even if, for the English, *Time's winged Chariot hurried near*, in his soul he knew that there was, underlying all things, no hurry. *So be it when I shall grow old, or let me die.* His lips formed each word affectionately under his fine moustache. Rafael would be back when he was ready. He had said that he would be away for a while and a while was now passing.

A lizard ran up the palings and paused at the top. It was pleasant to have the yard to himself, but he and Rafael would slot together again as naturally as two seeds in a pod. The yard suited them. Let the aunts and uncles hold court in the house, keeping up the good name of the Romeros. It was an old name and a respected one. He and Rafael were mavericks – Carlos too, but he was dead. Miguel managed the business now; Loloy had joined the police.

Without reaching for his book he found the middle

pages in his mind, the Thomas Hood, and heard the sonorous lines with his inner ear. There was a word he could ask Charles. Cowslip. He was not familiar with this but Charles would tell him about cowslip. The English-man was a comrade. The Americans in Manila had known many things and this Englishman, this professor of geology, knew even more. He appreciated a nice smoke, too. They had a cultural exchange.

Alphonse smiled. His thoughts moved on to Emma and re-played his encounters with her. The first time, at the tea party of Loloy's brother-in-law, whose daughter was a college student and her tutor was Charles. *What a tangled web we weave.* Emma, newly arrived and gleamingly pale, had appeared with Charles and Valerie. How the pieces moved over the chequerboard of life, forwards, sideways, black and white. This was an excellent image; he must make a note of it. Alas, though, it had already been used by Edward Fitzgerald in the *Rubaiyat*, page three hundred and forty something.

Manan's face had been a picture when she learned that the unexpected guests were not Americans, but English – and she with her portrait of the Queen above her bed all her life! The children had been in their Sunday clothes, all the girls with their hair in ribbons, all the aunts and cousins pressed into those tiny rooms, excuse me, excuse me. Eventually they had said their polite goodbyes and brought the English here to this very yard with a bottle of rum, and discussed Auden and Eliot all evening. It had been a meeting of minds. For the first time since he had lived in Manila he, Alphonse Romero, had been able to open his heart amongst those who understood.

What next? Next, another invitation to the house of Valerie and Charles. They were not married, they lived together like brother and sister; they were foreigners. The house had a flush toilet. Charles had a girlfriend from among his students, Fili. Emma was not his girl, she was a guest. She had travelled all the way alone and without a companion, yet she was as soft as a young coconut, as far as he could tell.

Alphonse shifted to his side, moved by the memory. He and Rafael had visited the house several times before the English had had their party. His mind skipped the party itself with its many impressions and went racing up the stairs into the big dark room and the girl beside whom he had lain so tentatively. Beside her twin full moons. She'd been drinking alcohol, she was a foreigner; he had kissed her mouth. She was tired – she also had something, an indisposition. Jet-lag. Culture shock. He was making sure that she was all right. She had let him touch her, here and there – it had been like stroking a sick animal, slightly sticky, slightly hairy.

A little later she had pushed him away, but not unkindly, he considered. She wanted to sleep. He had crept downstairs cautiously and found Rafael gone and the students also, but Charles, Valerie, the German tutor, and an American from Cebu were all lying down and listening to music. Alphonse could well remember, six weeks later, the unfamiliar song mixed with the buzz of the cicada outside. *And when the foghorn blows, I'll be coming home*, sang the man's voice.

He hummed now, turning again to lie on his back on the narrow bunk behind the washing line. He was just about to begin the next sequence, his tour of the forest with Emma, when he heard Rafael's whistle.

It was too hot on the patio in the afternoons. The children were gone from the path, the hens subdued in the yards, the whole island lay stunned by heat. Emma couldn't get into the habit of siestas; it was so difficult to sleep in the middle of the day. After lunch in the London office – a reality which slipped ever further away – there had always been a renewed push to finish early and to escape home ahead of the rush hour. Now there was no such hour, nothing to finish, and no escape. On the contrary, she urgently needed to make a start with her writing.

The noises from Charles' room also made an afternoon sleep impossible. He took Fili to bed for a couple of hours and their muffled, animal sounds were dreadful to hear from the other side of the partition; even downstairs Emma could follow the rhythms drummed out on the floorboards. She couldn't bear Charles sometimes. That Fili looked like a child of twelve, though he said that she was sixteen and had reached the age of consent. She was consenting, no doubt of that.

Emma covered her ears and wrote rapidly. *Bright light spatters/heavy lidded morning squirms/red hot night/black, black, utterly black/leaning nipa huts/white orchids/and endless sound like the sea.* She sighed. Apparently you just had to write, even if a story wouldn't come; you had to keep the pen moving across the paper, making word associations, anything. She tore off the page and began to write a letter to her mother. She would tell her that she had found her spiritual home.

Valerie came down the stairs, wearing a sarong and yawning. She didn't seem disturbed by the noises upstairs; she had a Thai boyfriend of her own and perhaps it didn't matter so much if you could do it too, Emma reflected. She thought of Alphonse. He was very sweet. Whenever they met he would nuzzle up and touch her, which was all right, but not in front of everyone. It would give the wrong idea. She noticed that Filipinos were demonstrative – people sat by the side of the road and picked over one another's scalps, young women walked along hand in hand. Men sometimes had whole conversations with their arms slung casually across each other's shoulders. Maybe Alphonse was behaving naturally and it signified nothing.

'Make us some tea, Em; be an angel.'

'Okay.'

'Been busy?'

'Oh. Yeah. Kind of.'

Valerie hitched one foot up into her groin and stood balanced on the other, her arms above her head and a smile on her face. She liked a bit of yoga after a siesta.

'Oh. Mm. Ah.'

'Sorry, no tea, I'm afraid. Electric's off again.'

'Okay. I'm off to change.'

Presently Fili came down, sliding through the room bashfully and vanishing through the open door. Charles came out of the shower rubbing his hair with a towel, lighting a cigarette and drawing a breath deeply and appreciatively into his lungs.

'Want a lift back to school, Val?'

'Sure. I'm meeting Toto about the play. You going now?'

'Oh... soon. You auditioning for the play, Emma?'

'Me? I don't think so. I'm not into that sort of thing.'

'Always a first time. One is here to experience, is one not? We thought *A Winter's Tale* under the palm trees might be rather enigmatic. Don't you think?'

'I've never wanted to do amateur dramatics, to be honest.'

'This isn't mere amateur dramatics, dear girl – this is east meets west, this is the riddle, the conundrum, the...' he spread his hands wide and dropped his voice. 'This is existentialism in the flesh.'

'Rubbish,' said Valerie, coming into the room. 'Leave her alone.'

'No, I mean every word – man must create values for himself by living each moment to the full – didn't he say that, that fellow, whatisname? Ask Alphonse, he'll tell you about it. Bring Shakespeare out here and you'll have the whole shoot. That's what I say, anyway.'

'Come on, then, shift yourself.'

'Right. Let's go.'

She couldn't ask Alphonse about existentialism, she hadn't seen him for a week. Perhaps this was just as well. If they didn't see each other then no one could consider them a couple. By no one, she meant his brother. She was uncertain about her own behaviour on the night of the house party, when everything had all been such a muddle. She'd only been in the country for a week or so – how could she know? She tried not to think of the neat brown hands gently roving across her stomach; she'd...

'Kumusta?'

She jumped up. She had heard no one coming. Framed in the doorway against the light was Rafael's short, stocky figure. He was lifted so exactly from her thoughts – leaning on the doorpost with his incongruous woolly hat, tapping his thigh with a papaya stem – she wondered for a moment if she had conjured him there.

'Kumusta ka?' he repeated. 'Charles? Valerie? Not here?'

'No...'

'I look for Alphonse. Not here, also?'

'No. Sorry...'

They stood still for a fraction of a second.

'Okay. Sorry I disturb you. Salamaat-a.'

He turned with a wave, crossed the patio, doubled back away from the road – she watched him through the fence – and disappeared into the trees.

She moved towards the table and fingered her half-finished letter. '*The people are so...*' She frowned and went into the kitchen, paused a moment. A cup, a knife, a spoon, a chopping board, a brown curl of onion skin, a gas bottle, a line of ants pencilled on the wall. She changed her mind and turned towards the bathroom, stopping halfway across the floor, her head on one side, listening. A little thread had worked its way into the house and was tugging at her, a tiny spider web pulling at her gut. She listened for a moment more, holding her breath, then abruptly left the house to follow him.

He was out of sight. Several minutes had passed and he might have gone one of several ways; the paths criss-crossed in all directions. As she started walking the tugging became stronger; she was quite sure of herself. The earth, trodden hard beneath many feet, felt warm. She had left her sandals behind. The palms rustled over her head. The thread pulled her on. Through a clearing, where a woman mashed something in a pot and a dog rooted in a pile of leaves, a rooster crowed and a basketball hoop hung askew on a pole. She nodded to the woman and walked on between the stilts of the huts, down the path on the far side. Oh, it was mad. It was mad and glorious. The path led to the sea.

She emerged from the trees and looked up and down the beach. There he was, five hundred yards ahead, walking along with his easy, rolling gait. The thread gave a final twitch and melted into the hot sky. Emma shaded her eyes and drew a deep breath. She could hardly trail him along the beach. She sat down in a corner of shade by an upturned boat and hugged her knees in amazement.

A week later she was jolting along on a bus, this time with Dolores from Colorado, America, in the next seat. She crept back into the memory of that strange impulse, imagining the thread as something gleaming and silvery drawing her through a strange forest in a strange land after a man – well, she hardly knew him. It had whispered something to her quite clearly: he is The One.

She wriggled with dread and joy, knocking Dolores on the elbow.

'Sorry.'

'Wassamatter?'

'Nothing. Where's this, d'you think?'

The bus had stopped again in a barrio, perhaps a town. Pepsi Cola signs rusted outside stores with their wooden awnings and inner darknesses. Dolores looked up from her magazine and shrugged.

'Dunno.' She turned the page.

Emma looked out at all the upturned faces. She could never do what this woman was doing, burying herself in *Time* or *National Geographic* while the world was out there and clamouring at the window. Ai mani! Ai mani! screeched the little boys. Guapa! A woman called to her. Guapa ikaw! The bus moved on.

How could anyone *read* when there was so much to see? Even inside the bus, the pennants and baubles hanging above the driver, the purple sheen on the sheets of hair in front of them, the scarlet blood on the hands of Jesus – it was all extraordinary. And out there – the broccoli canopy of trees and the flickering dark-green pools as the road plunged through those trees, the glint of rivers, the taste of the dust, the heat. Dolores turned another page.

'How can you do that?'

'What?'

'How can you read while we're going along? You're missing everything.'

'What? Where?'

'You know... everything.' She gestured left and right. 'You don't see that in Colorado, do you?'

'I guess not. Actually, Colorado would look pretty amazing to me right now. I've been here nearly two years, remember.'

'Not *here*, though.'

'In Baguio, then.'

'But you haven't ever been to *this* island – you've never been down this road in your whole life before.'

Dolores looked out doubtfully. 'It all kind of looks the same.'

'You're *tired* of it?'

'Well – let's just say that right now this article about the Alaskan oil fields seems a whole lot more interesting.' She looked at Emma's astonished face and laughed. 'Okay. You win. The oil fields can wait.' She tucked the magazine down into her bag. 'Happy now?'

Emma smiled. The green shadows sped by, the slanting eyes looked up. Superimposed on these, like images on a screen, she saw massive oil pipes stretched across snow. She dragged herself back into the here and now. It ought to be easy but she knew too much, there were too many layers in her head.

By the end of the day they were floured from head to foot in dust. Dolores had fixed a scarf over her head down to her eyebrows; Emma spat into a square of toilet paper as the bus roared into San Carlos and shook to a halt. They peered between the river of brown limbs, looking for a white face. His name was Ellis, apparently, this friend of Dolores – a Peace Corps worker, like herself. That was as much as Emma knew. Dolores had turned up in Dumaguete and stayed overnight on the way to visit this Ellis. You want to travel, don't you? Charles had said to Emma. Dolores would be glad of some company, wouldn't you, Dolores? Oh sure, she said. Sure. You're real welcome to come along.

'Well, I guess I figured he might not be here. We'll take one of these things. Hey! Isla sa San Carlos! O-o.'

The pedicab driver revved his engine, sending a fresh layer of dust over them. Just as Emma climbed into her seat she caught sight of someone out of the corner of her eye. Someone in the moving crowds of the market who was standing still, watching them. That same woman – surely it was? It couldn't be. Emma looked again.

'Buck up.'

'Oh. Coming.'

She wedged herself in, giving a yelp as the hot seat burned the back of her legs. She didn't look up, she fiddled in her bag for something until they had turned two or three corners and were suddenly alongside the sea. An island lay a mile or two offshore. Two jetties reached into the water, one concrete, against which a small pumpboat was moored, and the other a crumbling wooden structure. Their driver indicated an outrigger canoe into which a dozen people were loading an assortment of small animals. Sakayan, he nodded, the sun flashing on his cracked sunglasses. The ferry.

Dolores scrutinised Emma as they waited for the ferry to leave.

'You okay? You look kinda sick. You get seasick?'

'Oh no. I'm a bit queasy. It's the sun.'

'Maybe diesel fumes from that ol' bus.'

'Yes. Maybe.'

The sea was choppy and the air fresh. Despite the piglet trussed up in a rope bag at her feet, Emma revived. They were nearing a tropical island. It looked a little drab, but still, it was the real thing.

'Gee, how big is this place; about five ks?'

'It's not very big, is it?'

'Heck, no. I can't believe Ellis has been holed up here all this time.'

'What does he do?'

'Oh, his mandate is reef management, sustainable levels

of fish stocks and stuff. From his letters I'd say he was doing a sideline in hocus-pocus.'

'Hocus-pocus?'

'Yeah – you know. Reckons to write a book about it when he gets back.'

After a moment of uncertainty in the surf, the canoe ran up the beach on a little wave. Everyone was soaked. This is how Captain Cook arrived, thought Emma. I'm an explorer. The children who ran to the boat took one look at her, hooted with laughter and ran away again. The sun pressed down. They set off along a sandy path, of which there was only one.

There was a settlement elevated on poles around a clearing in the middle of the island, on sand. Sand everywhere, the entire island was sand. O-o, smiled a woman, pointing. Ellis! America! They could see the sparkle of water again a hundred yards away. The island was less than half a mile wide.

'That must be it.' Dolores indicated a hut facing the ocean. The Stars and Stripes could just be made out on a faded flag fluttering on the roof. 'Yup. Hope he's prepared a banquet.'

Above the doorway, on a string, a cluster of bones and shells jingled in the wind. There was no door. They peered in.

A jumble of pots, bottles, sticks; a guitar. A table, papers and books, a photograph of a dog and, on a platform like a bunk bed, a pile of clothing. Nobody.

'Guess he's out.'

'Should we go in, do you think?'

'Well, I for one am not sitting out here. C'mon. I need a drink.'

'Drink?'

'Water.' Dolores was opening bottles and sniffing. 'Phee-oo! There must be a well someplace. You sit down; you don't look so great. I'll be right back.'

Emma sat on the slatted floor. There was no space to lean against anything and her head was heavy. The bones and shells jingled and jangled outside. Her throat hurt when she swallowed. She was getting a cold.

Four

Dolores looked over the side of the bunk. Naturally she had taken the bunk, as she was the one who knew Ellis. She might even know him really well, but how well, Emma didn't like to ask. She had no compunction about going through his papers, anyway.

'Some of this stuff is really weird. Listen.'

Emma didn't listen. She lay scrunched up in a ball on the floor, hearing only the continuous whispering sound of the wind sifting the sand below. Dolores had said the night before that it might be something called dengue fever, since Emma had felt shivery, despite the heat. But it wasn't; it was a beastly cold. She had to use her shawl as a hankie, working her way around the edge, as there were no tissues. There was only water to drink when what she really needed was Lucozade. Ellis had not returned.

'Going by what he says here, I'd guess he's gone walkabout in Siquijor. Naughty boy, leaving his post.' There were voices outside. Ma'am! America ma'am!

'I'll see what they want.'

Dolores clambered down over Emma's head and ducked out of the hut. Emma heard her speak to someone and their voices grow indistinct. Shoof, shoof, went the wind through the sand. Jingle, jangle, went the bones. Her mother would have put her to bed with a hot water bottle. A few tears of self-pity ran down her face.

'Look – aren't they beautiful! Sorry, did I give you a fright? It's only me; who did you think it was?'

Two large fish lay draped across her arms. The tail of one of them gave a twitch.

'God! It's still alive.'

'Just about. Can't get them much fresher, hey? I'll make a fire. Dinner coming up.'

She let them slide to the floor and Emma heard her behind the hut, cracking wood. She looked at the fish in anguish. They were indeed beautiful, their purplish-green shine rapidly going dull. Their eyes stared up at her. The tail flipped again.

'Take them *away*,' she screamed.

'What?'

'Take them away. Put them back in the sea.'

'Beg pardon?'

'It's awful. They're dying. Put them back in the sea, for God's sake.'

'Are you crazy? I just paid a peso for those. They're beauties. Delicious.'

Emma rose unsteadily to her feet. Her limbs felt as if they

were glued together.

'Then I shall put them back.'

'Don't be silly.'

Dolores returned to her fire. Emma looked at the fish, which were still staring at her. She couldn't bear to touch them, ugh. Dolores returned and picked them up by their tails.

'You're going to cook them while they're still... alive?'

'Look, sweetie, these are *fish*. The sea's bountiful harvest. A gift from the Lord — that's what these people say. What the hell else do you suppose they eat?'

'Rice?'

'Oh, sure... rice. You see any paddy fields around here? Rice they must buy — it's cheap enough, but fish is free. Those boys are as happy as Larry because their fish earned them a peso. I got my dinner. Everyone's happy.'

'They're not.' Emma pointed unhappily. 'They're dying.'

'They've had a great life, honey. Don't mess with the ways of the world, you'll fall on your ass. Now, if you don't want to see them dispatched, you go off for a little toddle. Geez, you're something else, you really are.'

Emma moved away to a spit of sand around the curve of the beach, from where the hut with its ghastly preparations was no longer visible. Sorry, sorry, sorry, she apologised to the sea. She blew her nose terrifically into her shawl, which she still clutched in her hands, and realised that she felt a bit better.

By the next day her cold was almost gone. In London it might have taken weeks, even months, to clear, but here it had galloped through her system and left her wrung out and exhausted. She and Dolores moved around each other carefully, tidying up their cramped space, offering each other polite and vegetarian titbits. When the afternoon became a fraction cooler she announced that she might go for a walk.

'Sure. Sure, you do that.'

If the island was about two miles long and half a mile wide, she might, reasonably, walk right around it. If she kept to the edge of the sea she could hardly go wrong. And if she grew tired – not being fully herself yet by any means – she could reach the place where the ferry had landed and then just walk through the settlement again. She slung her bag across her shoulders, carrying her sandals and a bottle of water, just in case.

It was a relief to walk away from the accusatory smell of fish. Past the sandpit and over a pile of white, white rocks, the beach stretching emptily ahead. She imagined Rafael walking in the distance. A poem was coming into her mind – with each step the words seemed to pull up out of the sand. *A woman moves towards the beach, bare-footed on the narrow path.* Yes, that was it. She would capture the magic of that moment when the moon and tide had coalesced with her own fate. (It had been a full moon; she had checked.)

The air was quite fresh on the island's seaward side, the

sea itself ruffled into tiny points. Its brightness prickled her all over; she was sparkly, light-headed. She was walking the Kalahari, the Gobi desert, the great Australian outback. No one on earth knew where she was. She walked free and untagged along a deserted beach and it was the best feeling in the world. She hadn't eaten much lately and she was probably getting thinner, too.

The sun was now behind her instead of on the left. She had rounded the headland without noticing it and the mainland had come into view. At the same time, on the right, the dense green of the island was receding as the beach grew wide. It was no longer a beach, strictly speaking. The sand was grittier and shelves of flat pumice-like stuff broke through it, cracked and veined by long-dried rivulets of water. Perhaps it *was* pumice; the volcano Charles had visited wasn't far away. Or perhaps it was coral. Her own ignorance struck her as astounding for a moment, but what did it matter? Her soul was on track.

The flat stuff, whatever it was, hurt her feet. She stopped to put on her sandals and it was only then that she noticed the crabs. Two large, bright-red crabs crawled out of a crack no more than a yard away, waving ungainly claws at her. She hurried on. More crabs ran about on her left; she zigzagged to the right.

There were crabs everywhere. The ground was bleeding scuttling, scarlet crabs as big as her hand; bigger. She looked back. There were even more of them behind, between her and the beach. She broke into a run, hopping this way and that. Red crabs teemed out of the ground and from between the reedy tussocks sprouting here and there.

All at once there was a man in front of her, wearing threadbare shorts and nothing else, and carrying a long, curved knife. He beckoned and began to walk rapidly away on black, horny feet. He tracked without hesitation through the reeds, occasionally clearing his way with a quick downward stroke. Scimitar, thought Emma. Machete. No, parang. There was sand underfoot again and palm trees creaking overhead. Her guide made a brief gesture that she interpreted as final, and vanished as abruptly as he had appeared. She was on the edge of the settlement.

'I'm going to split tomorrow.'

'What? Oh.'

They were cross-legged in the hut, which groaned and stretched noisily in the wind. The avocado and rice mixture in their bowls was crunchy with sand. Everything was sand, the food, the water, the clothes, the bedding; also, Emma discovered, her toothpaste. The wind was rising. According to local gossip this was the tail of a typhoon, of which in the South China Sea there were many. Flicking their tails, in Emma's mind, like playful dragons.

'There's a bus up to Bacolod tomorrow. I don't need to go back to Dumaguete. You can stay here, if you want.' The wind drowned her words.

'Sorry?'

'Stay here IF YOU WANT.'

Emma looked at the heaving, shuddering walls in the twilight. Certainly not. 'Ellis might come back.'

'And be delighted to find you here. Come to think of it, he'll be lucky to find his hut here.'

All night the wind screeched through the slats. At first light Dolores packed her bag.

'I'll leave him a note, the schmuck. Fine host he's been.'

'Maybe he didn't intend...'

'Oh, men never *intend* anything.'

'You think the ferry will be running this morning?'

'I sure as hell hope so.'

It was not, but a large boat chugged through the waves, calming the surface slightly with its leakage of oil. They made no attempt to speak during the crossing, but covered their heads until they stood in the lee of the wind behind the nearest building on the mainland.

'Is it worth getting a pedicab?'

Emma shook her head; they knew the way and it wasn't far. Rounding the corner of the market she thought of the woman who had stood at the same spot, staring at her. She must have mistaken her; all the women looked very much alike with their small figures and straight black hair. She pushed the thought down, where it lay uncomfortably inside her, like a cream bun.

Dolores consulted her watch. 'Looks like your bus goes first. Must be that one. That's the one we came up on, isn't it?'

'What about you?'

'I'm going to find someplace to wash.' She wiped her cheek ruefully. 'I've been sandblasted all right. Are you getting in, or you got time for a Coke, or what? Bus won't be going anywhere for a while by the look of it.'

'I'll get in. Well. I suppose...'

'It's farewell, honey. Best of luck. See ya.'

She waited outside until Emma had sat down, then waved goodbye. Emma watched her go with misgivings; she wouldn't see her again, almost certainly not, not ever. Life was a huge sea and she floated through it, brushing against other lives like weeds in the current. At least she was out of the wind for a while. She looked around, sharply aware of being alone. After a minute she picked up her bag and moved to the very back of the bus.

'I know exactly what you have in mind. You're nurturing an idea....' Charles took a mouthful of beer and waved the bottle at her. 'An idea of shedding all the dross, all the horrors of society, going Fanti and staying here forever.'

'Going where?'

'Fanti. As in Kipling. Or was it Chesterton?'

Valerie threw a cushion at him.

'Stop showing off, Charles.'

'I am not; Emma must know what I'm referring to. I mean, to what I am referring – she's meant to be a writer, isn't she? And I'm not wrong; I know I'm not. I've seen it all before. I've felt it. It's part of our colonial make-up.'

'You're completely wrong, actually.' Emma felt her nose prickle, as it always did when she was trying not to cry. 'Quite the opposite, in fact. I don't in the least want to colonise.'

'Oh, but you do. You do.'

'Well, what about you?'

'Me? Oh, I'm not staying. I'm fulfilling my contract and then I'm off, thanks very much. With two years' experience in the field on my cv. Get myself a well-paid job, a house with all normal services as required by civilised man – ie, running water, choice of hot and cold – electricity supply that remains on all the time – bliss! And a car, and an intelligent wife with whom I can have conversations. In English. There.'

'What about Fili?'

'Fili? What about her? The white man's chocolate fantasy.'

'Emma, tell him to put a sock in it.'

He laughed. 'Sock? When did you last see a sock? Emma is taking me perfectly seriously, aren't you, darling?'

'And what about what *you've* learned here – what it's teaching *you*. You're the one who told me about the cultural exchange.'

'Not me. God forbid. That must've been Val. Where's she gone?'

'I'm out here. I'm on the patio. I'm not listening; you're a fatuous bastard. Take no notice of him, Emma.'

Emma looked at the page in front of her. She almost had it. She had had it on the bus, the whole poem perfectly, but her journal had been at the bottom of her bag and with all that bumping and jolting on the back seat she hadn't even attempted to write it down. Out of an entire poem she could now only recall the first verse. *The woman moves towards the beach, bare-footed on the narrow path. The palms sway slightly as she swings, light-stepping in the heavy noon.* It had the right mesmeric feel to it, the dense syllables conveyed a kind of inevitability. However, she wasn't sure about using two hyphens in one stanza. She doodled on the page. Bother Charles.

She was still doodling when a low whistle sounded on the path. Charles ambled towards the fridge. Sounds like more beers are needed, he said. Two figures stepped onto the patio. She kept her head down, pressing her knees together tight with happiness. It was Alphonse, definitely. And Rafael.

They hesitated at the door. Hello. Kumusta! Kumusta. Alphonse came to the table where she sat and dropped down beside her.

'You work? You write poem?'

'Oh, it's not finished.'

'I have one. I have some. I show you.'

He produced handfuls of lined paper from his shoulder bag and leafed through them with quick, eager movements. Emma hadn't looked at Rafael, except for a glance that had startled her with joy. It confirmed everything. The skin on her left side sensed him, over there in the corner with Charles and now moving towards the patio. She frowned, trying to concentrate. Alphonse had written these in English, after all. The least she could do was to read them properly.

'I like this one. And that. You write about the sea a lot.'

'O-o. As metaphor. The sea brings flotsam on the tide of injustice. And here, I use volcano. The forces erupt and there is conflagration.'

'That's wonderful, Alphonse. I could never do that in Visayan.'

'No, no. It's nothing. I lack the words.'

'Alphonse! Beer! Come on out here, you two.'

They sat in the dusk, swatting at mosquitoes. Rafael leaned against the low wall, his face under the woolly hat hidden in shadow. Charles' tobacco tin was open at his side.

'Rafael tells me you've been hatching a plot, Alphonse.'

Rafael whistled. 'No plot. Just ideas, only.'

'We have ideas of going out.'

'Oh yes?'

'By the 'back door'. You know this way?'

Charles nodded. 'I heard about it. Into Borneo?'

'O-o.'

Valerie passed a joint to Charles. 'What's this about Borneo?'

'You know, they can't get passports.'

'We can, now. Officially. Pero, very expensive, no?'

'It is like saying we cannot leave – it is the same. The government say: you can have passport. It look good to say this. But it cost thousand of dollar. Thousand. Who has thousand?'

'You go from Mindanao?'

'Some go. From Zamboanga in a boat it is not so far. But there are pirates.'

'And when you arrive in Borneo without papers? What then?'

Alphonse shrugged. 'This is talk, only. That's all. Maybe, is impossible. We go to Mindanao. Who knows?' He turned to Emma. 'You come with us also, no? You want?'

'Me? To Borneo?'

He wagged his head, laughing. 'No, no, no. We stay in Mindanao for visit with cousins. A good place. Far far. No flotsam. You come, tomorrow.'

'*Tomorrow?*'

'Why not?' He beamed. 'We take the boat, six o'clock. Twelve pesos. Filipina-ka. You will learn all Visayan and write a big book, okay? Daghan poema.'

'Okay. Yes, I'll come. Six o'clock in the evening?'

'Sus! Buntag, na lang. In the morning. We will arrive here for you. Muabot akog sayo. Is okay?'

'Is okay.'

Charles let out a cheer. 'We'll drink to that. Wait a minute, who needs a refill? Shit, there's only two left. We'll share. Here. To the spirit of – what? To the crossing of The Great Divide?'

Five

Alphonse stepped briskly along. This had been a good idea, a flash of inspiration. Emma had been on an excursion already in the company of the American lady, which had not been a great success, by all accounts. Her pioneering spirit had not been allowed full rein, or her creativity. He sympathised. His was a similar nature. Now she would travel with him. Now he would introduce her to everyone.

It was barely light, and still cool. They would walk to the harbour along the beach rather than through town; there was no need to make their departure too public. Having decided this to his satisfaction he turned across the culvert with his mind emptied. It was necessary to walk with an empty mind sometimes. To be aware of the decreasing darkness. To smell the breakfast fires on the morning air. To hear the roosters crow.

He stood at last outside the English house. The door was locked, which was momentarily unsettling. He whistled.

Tapped softly. It opened and there she was, smiling with excitement and a trace of anxiety. Was she ready? She thought so. She had her Kolget? He patted his back pocket, turning to show her the tube of toothpaste there. Toothpaste, she said. In England we have not just Colgate, but many kinds. Oh, never mind.

She closed the door quietly behind her and followed him along his zig-zag route, while he explained that they could better appreciate the dawn by walking along the beach. She nodded.

The wharf was a black mass against the sky in which a gash of scarlet was opening wider every second. It was like a mouth with the bright teeth of clouds, now pink, now bronze.

'*The sanguine sunrise, with his meteor eyes, and his burning plumes outspread*. Our friend, Shelley. Is it not so, Emma? Emma?'

'Mm? Sounds like him, yes.'

Emma was looking at the figures standing here and there on the dock. He had said 'we', hadn't he? He had definitely said '*We go to Mindanao*'. And: 'You come with *us*'. She was sure of it. He had also said '*We* will come for you' – and yet he was alone this morning. She looked about. Wasn't Rafael coming, then? Had there been a change of plan? Had she misunderstood?

Alphonse took Emma's money into the harbour office and after a moment beckoned her inside. Could she spell her family name, please? The clerk signed the ticket with a flourish and a look of frank admiration in her direction. Alphonse took her arm. 'Come. We embark already.'

The *Victoriano* lay peacefully at her berth, touched by the sun, the movement of men across her gangplank picked out along their edges in gold, like a Christmas card. Emma gazed back along the coast road, the harbour road; the beach. No Rafael. Alphonse led her to the middle deck, away from the funnels. It was best to be amidships.

'Gidagat-on? You have nausea in the ship?'

'Do I get seasick, you mean? No?

'Seasick? Good. Gidagaton. Seasick.'

'Do you?'

'No.'

The noises of the engines sounded from somewhere below.

'What time is it?'

He proffered his bare wrist. 'Time? Time is an illusion.'

'Oh – I just meant, will we be leaving soon?'

'Ah, English! This English concept, na lang. But yes, probably. Why not?'

'Can we watch?'

She sometimes showed an obstinate side, he reflected. He had elected to sit here, to contemplate the sea and the dawn, the latter already far advanced. To take in the prospect of an unsullied world before the journey across those very waters. But she had disappeared to the landward side of the ship. Also, leaving her bag behind. He regretfully picked it up with his own – they would lose their places –

and joined her at the opposite rail. She was studying the quay intently.

'Look. They're casting off.'

'O-o. See, it is six o'clock, or it is not six o'clock. Nevertheless – we go! Come. We find our places.'

The deck was becoming crowded. They stepped over legs and bundles and found a small space, Emma removing her sandals, putting them in her bag, sitting in the scuppers and dangling her feet over the side. Funny English. In the movies they did not do such things. But, there was also much common ground. Now, for instance, they discussed the million drops of water churning below, an inestimable number of drops making up this ocean and all the oceans between here and her own country. This very drop – or that one – might once have thrown itself upon those far shores, once upon a time. It stretched the mind, to consider such things.

They were studying the water when Rafael found them. Emma was visibly startled; her neck and then her face flushed very red. A blush. Alphonse had never seen one before. After that she stared with even deeper concentration into the sea, and out towards the horizon.

They played cards. She could play rummy, she said, but would not, just now. They played on the deck while she continued to gaze meditatively about. Ruminantly, he thought, the English word presenting itself as he transferred a run of sevens to the front of his hand. Ruminant, the fatted calf. Ruminant, ruminate, rummy. His English was improving by leaps and bounds, merely by being in her company.

He had chosen their places for a reason, as Emma now saw. The afternoon sun was on the starboard side, leaving them, on the port side, with some shade. She lay, like everyone else, flat on the deck, but she was awake, her hat tipped at an angle to shield her eyes from the reflected light. The engines rumbled on and on below. Alphonse lay asleep at her side and Rafael, a few feet away, lay with the upper half of his face covered by a folded handkerchief. The relief of seeing him surged through her again. She was replete with it; she needed nothing more.

An empty bottle of San Miguel beer rolled slowly by. She and Alphonse had shared it at lunchtime; they shared a great many things. She looked at him with affection. He was easy company; a good friend.

The meal below decks had been a boisterous business, what she had seen of it. She had glimpsed a great mound of rice and a crowd of men tucking in with their fingers, and then Alphonse had hustled her away. She was better off on the open deck with the other ladies and children, eating their own provisions. Alphonse brought her a plate of rice. 'Good I said: bring a fork with you, no? Fork, tenedor. Plate, plato. Saucer, platito. Okay?'

The rice was as white as snow and glued together into lumps. She hadn't eaten white rice for ages; nobody would *think* of it back home, where all her friends ate brown rice, preferably organic. Here they fed brown rice to the chickens. It was all very strange, she thought, giving herself up to the warmth of the deck. Very strange, and quite wonderful.

A thin line edged across the horizon towards late afternoon.

'Landfall,' she said.

'Fall? You say, the land *fall*?'

'Landfall. It's all one word, I think. It means to approach land. Like we are.'

He stroked his moustache. He and Rafael both had moustaches, which on Alphonse looked trim, setting off his dark eyes and black hair. On Rafael the effect was altogether different. Rougher. His skin was pockmarked from old pimples and his hair, not quite straight, stuck out from beneath his hat. His cheekbones were broader, his nose flatter, like an Oriental. He *was* an Oriental. They all were. She tended to forget. She touched her own cheeks, where there was no shape at all, really.

But what was she thinking of? Here they were, making landfall, watching the green coast of Mindanao unroll out of the sea, an apparently impenetrable mass of trees. Their ship veered round the headland towards a small harbour and the noise of her engines abruptly stopped. The silence was filled by the rattling of anchor chains.

'What's happening?'

'Umbot. Usa pa. Wait.'

Emma was left alone, pinned against the rail in a sudden

flurry of activity on deck. Towards the bows a rusty lifeboat was being winched jerkily towards the sea. Everyone seemed to be shouting. Alphonse reappeared at her side.

'Is okay. Nothing is the matter. This boat cannot – you know, get tied up? We use lifeboat.'

'Lifeboat?'

'Is okay. You can jump. Not far. This way.'

He led Emma forward, where the crowd melted aside at the sight of her white face. No – you first, she tried to indicate, but he took her hand, stepping carefully over sacks of rice and panniers of hens. Excuse, excuse! At the gap in the rail he took her bag.

'Okay. I go first.'

She peered after him over the edge. The lifeboat rose and fell on the surge a few feet below, while men took the strain at the ropes fore and aft and a foamy space gapped between the two vessels, closed and gapped again. Alphonse looked up.

'Come. Is okay. Jump.'

She jumped. Helping hands guided her to a seat; the boat was almost full. Excited shouts came from all sides, more people jumped, children were lowered, crates, boxes, sacks. Another engine roared. In a few minutes they were unloading at the harbour.

Emma looked around. It was smaller than Dumaguete, just a few buildings, shacks, and a road bending uphill into trees.

'What is this place?'

'Dipolog. Come. Hurry. We must run.'

At the corner a bus stood with engine running, like an animal ready to pounce. They clattered on board and took seats at the back. She hadn't seen Rafael since the boat but there he was, restored by some uncanny magic, a few seats away. The two brothers didn't necessarily sit together. Well, why should they? It was only in her English mind that there was anything odd about it. It suggested discord, but there was none. On the contrary, an almost palpable accord existed between them. It struck her that Rafael might be leaving them alone together on purpose.

'So.' Alphonse smiled genially. 'Here is Mindanao.' Emma remembered its shape from a map, the most southerly island and the largest. Named after a princess. As they hurtled along the road she had the impression that it was wilder, the vegetation denser. Perhaps the rapidly approaching dusk made it appear so.

'We're going awfully fast.'

'O-o. Maybe road blocks at night. Hold on.'

She grabbed the back of the next seat just as the bus jolted over a hole, bumping her into the air.

'Wow. I nearly hit the ceiling. How do you mean, road blocks?'

'Sometimes rebels. Insurgents.'

'Insurgents against what?'

'Of course, the government.'

She held on tight. The bus swung on through the

darkish land and its heavy scents, coconut palms against the sky, bridges, rivers, the glimpse of a boat, more trees, faster and faster, apparently along the very brink of something. It was quite dark when they arrived. Somewhere. She walked with them through streets of squat buildings, stopping where a light spilled out across the pavement. In here, we eat. Gigotum ako. I'm hungry. Pagkaon, food.

They sat at a tiny table under a fluorescent light and its attendant moths. Plates and tumblers on the table were turned upside down on a plastic cloth. Rafael went to a door at the back, spoke to somebody, and returned with two cigarettes, offering one to Emma. When she shook her head he crossed his index fingers with a look of inquiry towards his brother, who nodded. Putting one in his hat, and replacing the hat on his head, he lit the other, took a long draw, and handed it across the table.

After rice and eggs and beer, they each drank a tumbler of water and went out into the dark. I am nowhere, thought Emma. I am nowhere with any name and even if I knew the name it would still mean nothing. There are no points of reference, only these two men, and to them I speak my own language slowly and in its simplest form. Everything is being cut away. I am beginning to be alive.

Along the black street, hardly a street, lit so irregularly that the stars shone vivid overhead. A dog lay stiff in a ditch; others nosed in the corners and ran away at their approach. A group of men sat on the porch under a lamp, playing chess. Buildings became fewer, raised on poles above the ground with wooden steps and picket fences. The sound of surf along a beach came out of the dark.

'Is here.'

She began to follow Rafael up the steps, but Alphonse murmured to her: wait. Two children issued from a doorway above and scampered across the verandah, passing her with subdued shrieks of excitement. A youth followed, his eyes showing white in the darkness. Rafael called to them softly.

By the light of a lantern she saw faces smiling at her apprehensively. The talk was punctuated by a low and unintelligible stream of words from a woman behind a screen. A bottle was produced on a tray, the tumblers upside down. Emma was offered a seat on a bench, though not a drink from the bottle. She sat smiling back from the semi-shadows. Smiling, smiling. It was all she could do. She scratched at her leg: one of the old bites had opened up again and felt sticky. Damn. Her ankles were an awful mess.

Alphonse lightly touched her arm. 'Sige na. All fix up. There is a room; Marcelina will take you.'

'Now?'

'O-o.' He waved his hand. 'Go with her. Then we will look at the moon.'

Emma followed the small figure of the woman, who carried a candle. Behind a bamboo screen, past a table and through an opening in the wall, there was a short bunk and a pillow in a space the size of a cupboard. The woman pointed, nodding. Emma put down her bag. Right. Sala-maat.

She supposed that Alphonse meant her to rejoin him. Cautiously she felt her way in the dark past the table and back to the room with the lantern and the smiling faces. Alphonse and Rafael were not there. She paused uncertainly. At the doorway she tried their whistle; hoo-hwee. From the undergrowth below came the response.

'Come, Emma. We visit the moon, no? Bulan.'

'Hang on a minute. I need a toilet.'

She ducked into the darkness of a bush. It was tricky business, letting this need be known. Their English was so good – even Rafael, who said little, apparently understood her well enough. But needing a wee had no easy colloquial term, as far as she knew.

She shuffled among the leaves and went back to the silhouette waiting on the path. Other figures politely made way for her. Gabii. Bii. Goodnight, goodnight. Rafael was not among them.

She and Alphonse followed the sound of the waves. The moon indeed shone full over the sea, fat and yellow as a ripe fruit.

'Katahum. Beautiful. *She drifts in a place of mystery while the earth ebbs and flows.*'

'Who wrote that?'

'Oh, a famous poet. Alphonse Romero.'

She laughed. 'Look! My God. Look at this.' The sea

broke at their feet in a scattering of greenish light. 'Is it phosphorescence? I've never seen it before.'

'Sure. Phosphor. The birthplace of stars.'

'You are a real poet tonight.'

He slipped an arm around her waist and she wriggled away.

'Just friends, Alphonse.'

'O-o. Friends.'

Squatting down, he wrote their names in the sand in the moonlight. 'Alphonse Romero. Emma Clarke. Friends in phosphorescence.'

In the morning she awoke to feel his hand gently laid on her head. Uh-ee. The precious sleep had hardly been enough; the sand on her feet had bothered her, as had the snoring and shuffling of unseen strangers behind the wall. She had also been disturbed by a chicken landing on her stomach. But now she rose quickly and dressed in the dark.

It was an hour or so before dawn. She had no idea where Alphonse had slept, let alone Rafael, but she accompanied him now outside without question. The darkness was sharp and crackling; there was no longer any moonlight. They walked along a road, a beach, a pier, into the town of Oroquieta. The name signified nothing; it was just a pretty name.

In a market already bustling in the dawn light they bought food for breakfast – eggs, onions, tomatoes. Piles of fruit or vegetables she did not recognise; laid out in baskets along the pavement. He told her their local names and shrugged. In English? He didn't know. There was no word. Such things did not exist in English.

The kitchen, in which she had squeezed past the table the night before, was visible for the first time in the morning sun through the planking of the wall. Rafael stood tending a fire. A pot of water steamed over a grill and he gave her a cup of something hot.

'Chicory. Good?'

She took the cup from his hand. It was a state of grace, wanting him.

Six

When Nanay Litong first heard the boys shouting the news about visitors on the way, she was nonplussed. A white visitor, she heard them say. The last white person to visit Sibukay had been Father Delaney on his pastoral call two years before, and before that, an American gentleman from Davao who had come up with ideas for a golf course in the foothills. Stakes driven into the ground for measuring purposes on that occasion were still there; she herself tied the pig to the one nearest her own yard, from time to time.

She hailed the smallest of the boys who had lingered in the hope of something from her kitchen. O-o, he said. He had seen it with his own eyes. Two men, whom Pablo had recognised as the sons of the Romeros of Dumaguete, were at this moment walking up the hill and between them was a white woman, with legs this big. His small brown hands indicated roughly the width of a banana tree. He looked up at Nanay earnestly and she pushed a sweet into his hand.

The Romero boys, and a woman. She shook her head, pushing back the grey hair that had come undone in the process, and called to her husband. As barrio captain he must be told; he must come to the gate to receive their guests. Eh! A room would certainly be needed; she would send Pablo to sweep the stairs, she would shake out the mats herself. Pablo! Another sack of rice! Kerosene! Pablo!

A thin, languorous youth appeared on the patio. Hup! she scolded. The broom, quickly! The stairs. The spare room. The leaves out there on the ground by the gate, quick! Quick! Pagdali!

Tatay Litong was amused to see his little wife in action. After a poke in the ribs from her he went back to their own bedroom where he had been having a little post-siesta, and changed his extremely worn and comfortable vest for a barong-tagalog with embroidered panels. His iron grey hair, kept in the American crew-cut style, required no attention, so he wandered through the gate and stood waiting at the top of the hill.

He could see a knot of people on the road, which ran with a slight curve through the tall palms. There were always people on the road, walking in one direction or the other, nothing unusual about that. He couldn't see who it was at that distance. His eyesight wasn't what it was. He waited.

Slowly they came into view. Two of the Romero boys and, confirming the squeals of the children, a white woman. An American! Tatay's heart swelled at the thought of the Americans. He put his hand out and found his wife's shoulder next to his, as he knew he would.

The woman was dressed like a man. Her hair was flat against her head and the colour of tallow; her face, like the priest's, was a high pink colour. Vicente and Rosa appeared from their house next door at the same summons from the little ones, but the Romeros came straight on up the hill to greet him, the captain, first.

It was Rafael, his niece's eldest. And his brother, Alphonse. They had no professions, these two; they were drifters, it was said. But all relations were welcome, very welcome. They raised his hand to their foreheads in respect, then Nanay's hand, then Vicente, then Rosa. They hailed their cousins. The woman stood squinting in the sun and smiled politely as they introduced her. My uncle. My aunt. My cousin. Their son. With her they shook hands, after her own custom. She smiled again and then went back to gazing over their heads up the hill where the road ended, and down, from where they had just come, and all around, in a kind of wonder.

Naturally, she would stay with them. Any foreigner in the barrio would be a guest in his house, built as it was to the western ideal. It was spacious, for one thing. The floors were of concrete downstairs and there was an enamel bath, although no water ran into it, as such. The water butt in the yard was perfectly good, and filling the buckets kept the boys out of mischief. There was a clock in the hall, the hands of which had stood at twenty past four for as long as anyone could remember.

'Come! Eat!' called his wife, making scooping movements with her hand and pointing to her mouth. Rafael
shook his head, reassuring her. They had eaten already in
the market in Ozamis, not to worry. Okay na lang. They
conferred for a moment before Alphonse took up Emma's
bag and inclined his head towards the house.

It was morning. Emma sat on the verandah, on a seat with
a plastic cover that was crisp and cracked around the edges.
The view was framed – smothered, really – in deep jungle.
Big leaves pushed in all directions from trees the genus of
which she didn't know; their green tongues stuck out in a
kind of careless profligacy. More leaves lay at her feet. A
cockerel, possibly the one which had mightily roused her
from her sleep several times during the night, scratched in
the earth a few feet away before shaking his glossy neck
and swelling his throat for another cry, his round eye fixed
upon her.

Her journal lay open on her knee. Her hand still hurt
from sea-urchin spines in Oroquieta; Alphonse had warned
her but she hadn't known that the reef was so near the
surface. The sea had been as clear as glass. She was afraid to
emerge from her swim, for a big crowd had gathered on
the sand to watch the white woman in a bathing suit. She
was audacious, bordering on the unseemly. Alphonse had
laughed and said: be careful of those, pointing down into
the water. Sea urchins? O-o, the black ones. Then her hand
had brushed against one and the spines broken off under

her skin. Urine, he said. You must use urine on it. Walking up the sand in front of her audience, crawling into the bushes with as much dignity as she could muster – it was embarrassing just to think of it. But so much had happened since.

She squeezed her hand painfully around her pen and began to write. '*No way will I go back to the world of the Tottenham Court Road after this. The bus to Ozamis, then we sat pouring sweat in the plaza, up to the 'village', touch hands to foreheads. Supper outside, walk the black hill in darkness, bring out a guitar and we sing as loud as we can. The night alive with sounds and stars. The second morning on the verandah, upturned coconut pieces on the road, hens, children, a silent sky rises out of clear white clouds. How very much I love him, and cannot let it out – I am the stranger; remind me of my place...*'

Soft footsteps sounded on the floor behind her and she hurriedly turned the page. It was Pablo, the houseboy. He sidled through the door, flicking his shining hair, a toothpick in his wide, exquisite mouth. He laid a hand on the verandah rail for a moment and folded long limbs to look around the corner, then unfolded in one movement out of the gate.

Emma shut her book. It wasn't clear what was expected of her now, if anything. Another English concept, Alphonse might say. Very likely nothing was expected of her, which was hardest of all.

They had had breakfast soon after sunrise. At the back of the house outside the kitchen door, seated around a table

with Nanay and Tatay and an indecipherable number of
cousins and neighbours and members of the household,
she had eaten rice. Saucers of vinegar, saucers of onion,
tomato, fish. The men had each tackled huge mounds of
rice, a spoonful of vinegar and tumbler of water, and risen
immediately. One by one they had disappeared, even
Tatay, who had grunted at her throughout the meal in a
concerned and friendly way, seeming much taken with
trying to set the machinery of his spoken English into
motion. Even Tatay had gone about his business. She alone
had none.

In the kitchen Nanay was chiding a clutch of small
boys as if they were hens. At Emma's attempts to offer help
she shook her head vehemently, flapping her apron. Of
course Emma could not do anything. So she retired to the
verandah to look purposeful with a pen and paper, and to
look out on paradise.

Alphonse found her there sometime later, and her pensive
face filled him with remorse. He should not leave her
alone, even if she declared that she liked it. He should not.
In his chosen role as protector and friend (if not more), he
should remain close by. Last night – also the night before
– he and Rafael had been reacquainting themselves with
comrades and some fine rum. Naturally. He was aware of
something which Emma could not know. In Dumaguete it
was possible for an English girl to drink and smoke and
whatnot – it was a town, they had seen the behaviour of

foreigners before. But not here. Here in the provinces the girls did not go out at night and sit with men and do such things. He was perhaps the only one to consider this. He stroked his chin, where he was growing a straggly beard. Delicate handling. Sige. Wala problema.

'Buntag, Emma. Kumusta?'

'Oh, hi, Alphonse. I'm fine.'

'Maayo man. I say: kumusta? And you say: maayo man, fine. You find a good place for writing, no?'

'Yes. But my hand still hurts.'

He took her hand and studied it with care. Little bumps had swollen on the pads of her fingers, punctured by tiny black specks.

'Is okay. In time, this will come out. You sleep okay?'

'Yes. Where did you sleep?'

'Here also. I was up early-early. Following the dawn. We go now. Bring your clothes.'

'My *clothes*?'

'O-o. We do laundry.'

On the balcony of the house opposite, Rafael sat waiting for them with a bowl piled high with clothing. The three of them set off down the road, passing a huge ox-like animal yoked to a cart, a small boy perched astride its neck and tapping it with a twig. Chrrp, murmured the boy. Fwh. Fwh. Chrrp. Obediently the animal swung to one side and lumbered off into the trees.

'Buffalo?'

'Carabao.'

'Caribou? Surely not?'
'Carabao. Very strong. And … kuan? Docile.'

Halfway down the hill an old lady moved along with small steps. Their grandmother. In her hand she held a leathery leaf of dried tobacco. When their greetings interrupted her thoughts she first eased herself down onto a nearby log and then lifted the leaf to her mouth like a bugle. She inhaled, squinting at them with cloudy eyes. Who was this? Romero? O-o. Perhaps she knew who they were, perhaps not. Then she noticed the stranger, a woman who was not a member of the clan by any stretch of memory or imagination. Americana. She peered more closely, running a finger along the stranger's arm. 'Sus, it was as hairy as a pig.

The old lady's touch was like contact with a distant planet. Not of this world as Emma knew it, yet she was undoubtedly their grandmother. Rafael had those cheek-bones; the mark of her face was on his, exactly. They left her sitting on the log, erect and remote with her smouldering leaf.

Water gushed out of the hillside and over a rock, a hundred yards from the road. A group of people squatted there, stirring clothes in the water or beating them on the stones. The bushes were dotted with washing; children jumped from pool to pool. The spray was full of rainbows.

Rafael set to work at once, selecting a place on a flat rock. Alphonse gestured to Emma: go on, after you.

'I don't know what to do.'

'Do? Come. I have soap. See.' He produced a thin block of blue soap, dipped a shirt into the pool and rubbed one energetically with the other. 'See. Easy na lang, no?'

It was easy. It was absolutely the right way to do the laundry. Water ran freely from the ground, the sun shone freely in the heavens. I've been out of touch with what is real for so long, she thought. All my life. It's my own fault. I'll never use a washing machine again.

How curious that things should change so quickly. A glancing blow from fate, a little nudge, and she faced a completely new direction. It was increasingly certain. There, in a small pool not five yards away, was the man she loved. It rose up in her like a shout, a lovely thing to be thrown high in the air for everyone to see, to be sung out loud. She bit her lip, and kept it down.

Seven

After a week in Sibukay – but already the relentless loop of weeks, seven days after seven days, had begun to loosen and disconnect – they decided to visit a small settlement in the mountains. Gala. The brothers reached the decision without Emma. How could she follow the rapid sentences between them, or between them and Nanay and Tatay, and everyone in the barrio? She didn't even try. A few words here and there were enough. They were going to a place called Gala; it was far, a day's walk maybe; they would set off before sun up.

Uh-eee. Wake up, Emma. Wake up.

The cockerel shrieked harshly outside but already the household was up and dressed, the houseboys holding a lamp over their packs, and re-adjusting their weight. 'Sus! fussed Nanay. A little more dried fish, there. Bring back oranges, yes, and cabbages. An exchange of goods. Send greetings. Behave yourselves. Take care of the Englandaka.

They called goodbye, setting off up the road in the papery

dark, settling the packs on their backs. Alphonse and Rafael each carried a sack of rice and some water; Emma had her own rucksack. They took up a fast pace at once and she had to quicken her steps. Sibukay was out of sight.

There was a rough track, the trees on either side huge black hulks; the stones at her feet becoming visible as the grey light increased. It was pierced suddenly by a shaft of orange; she turned and saw the sun on the lip of the tree-tops. But she lost a second in looking back, and hurried again to catch up. The light ran down the slopes like the top of a tin peeling off. It lit the mud holes under the trees, the carabao lifting their slow heads, birds skimming from cover to cover. The path grew steeper. The brothers kept walking.

She wanted to say: look at that! Look at that insect, that flower, that view! It seemed a pity not to; she knew how to appreciate a walk in the great outdoors. But there was no breath to spare for talking. The men hadn't exchanged a word since they set off. They shared a rhythm, their breathing and walking, the same. Only now it was more like climbing.

The track was the bed of a small river, now dry, its banks increasingly steep, its pebbles sometimes rocks, even boulders. These made for pauses, and a handing up of the packs, but always the steady pace resumed, on and on.

It was getting very hot. She needed to stop pretty soon. She shifted the bag on her shoulders. The shoulders in front of her, Alphonse's, were wet with sweat. She was too tired to see anything else. Just hot, wet shoulders, swinging easily from side to side, part of the landscape, the brownness and the heat.

Suddenly they stopped, though no one had spoken. They smiled at her. Okay? We stop. Tubig. Water. They unslung a bottle and drank, while she sank down gratefully. She sat on her sandals as she had seen the men in Sibukay do, airing her hot toes. Whew. That was great. She never knew she could walk like that. The brothers did not sit; Alphonse packed the water bottle away and Rafael wandered into the bushes. In a moment he was back and at once made a brief lifting gesture with his hand. Come. We go on.

It was harder to start again, even after so short a rest. Her legs trembled a little. They set the pace, steadily up and up, side to side. They're testing me, she thought. They're testing the English woman to see how soft she is. But I'll keep up with them. They'll see that I can.

Twice they stopped in the same way, for two minutes and a drink of water. The men dropped the packs, lifted their T-shirts, wiped their faces, grinned. She felt her own face swollen and only slightly moist. She couldn't sweat properly; it was a nuisance. She just heated up like a pressure cooker. She could hardly see.

Alphonse had been carrying her pack as well as his own for a while but even so, by the third stop she was winded. She blew and snorted but her breath refused to come and go regularly. Her lungs were damp, useless balloons. She peered at Alphonse. The climb had apparently affected him quite differently; he seemed to have eaten the air. He was nourished by it and joyful, honed as a racehorse. She glanced at Rafael. The same.

The sun lost its vertical grip as they left the river bed and came out to the open slopes. The hilltops that had been hidden in the cloud were now ranged around them, and a few shacks. Gala. There was the farm of Benito, the barrio captain. There's only one farm? she asked, looking around. No. There are others, one or two, here and there. Alphonse waved his arms in a wide circle. There were no other buildings in sight. Benito himself moved towards them in the distance, on a path that dipped and disappeared into the cloud and out again.

A few goats watched their approach. Rafael whistled at the house fence, and called. Emma straightened her back. The air, so high up, was fresh. She felt a little drunk.

A young woman appeared in the doorway, looking surprised. Rafael climbed the steps and spoke rapidly. O-o. She waved them in. It is Lita, Benito's wife, said Alphonse. She has no English.

Inside there was one room, a sleeping quarter to one side and a cooking area leaning against the house. Lita spread her hands and the brothers nodded. Of course. We can sleep on the floor, of course. Together. Is okay.

You have the big climb, no? Alphonse sat next to Emma on the top step. I have the big climb, yes, she nodded, laughing. I feel better now. Bitaw, he replied. The mountain air is for the soul. Where do you learn these things,

Alphonse? He put his head on one side and smiled ambiguously.

I wonder if he will mind, she thought. I wonder if he will mind that I love his brother. He is always the one who is with me. Now, for instance, Rafael has vanished again. He just goes off, on his own, while Alphonse stays and looks after me. Is he being discreet, leaving us alone like this? But Alphonse doesn't treat me as a lover – it's not like that. Only that one time. Oh, I'm sure he won't mind. Love can't be wrong. And Rafael? He gives no sign. I will say nothing, will show as little as I can; I can do nothing.

In the evening she stretched out on the slats of the floor, her limbs wonderfully heavy, sinking downwards and leaving another part of her to float. The soul, maybe, of which Alphonse had spoken. He lay near her, but not too near. They spoke quietly, of this and that, looking up into the dark thatch of the roof while their hosts moved behind the curtain, shushing the baby. Rafael had not come back.

Unforgettable, that's what you are
Unforgettable, though near or far

She woke suddenly, her arms and legs stiff, pinning her to the floor. A voice had burst into her sleep. Rafael? Singing Nat King Cole?

It's incredible
That someone so
unforgettable

There was a flourish of flamenco and a laugh. Alphonse stirred and lifted his head. Ouf. They are serenading you, he said. They are drunk. Emma could hear the smile in his voice.

She awoke a second time, just before light. It was excruciating to move, but she needed a wee. Rafael lay against the wall with a shirt over his face, snoring softly. She crawled to the doorway, eased herself down the steps and down the path to the bushes, then back again, lying down between them. She was aware of love, and the wonder of it, and the sound of Lita nursing the baby, before she fell back to sleep.

He was in the cooking area, coaxing the embers of the fire, first thing in the morning. He gave her a sheepish smile and perhaps a wink; she wasn't sure. His eyes, always bloodshot, were more so. The woolly hat was over his ears.

'Bugnaw sa buntag. Cold, no?'

'Yes. Lovely.'

'You like? You like cold? Sige na. You have cold like England, no?'

'Yes.'

'Sorry I disturb your sleep.'

'It was nice. Good singing.'

'Good singing, ha? True?'

'True.'

Alphonse joined them, tousling his hair. Rafael carefully fed the fire and balanced over it an iron pot.

'First I make... kuan?' He asked Alphonse to translate a word. 'Okay. I make: ginger. Ginger, no? Make hot.' He rubbed his stomach. 'Make warm. Good.'

She watched. Alphonse brought firewood and husks of coconut while Rafael managed the flames under the pot, bending down, blowing gently. She could stretch out her fingers and run them down his back. She sat mesmerised, not doing so. He chopped ginger root with a knife, crushed it, added sugar, stirred. He handed her a cup. Oblation, she thought, catching the word out of nowhere. Oblation, ablution, absolution. This keeps happening. It's a kind of madness. I'm so happy.

While the rice cooked they went out to look for the stream. Benito had gone to the fields long before; Lita was milking the goats, the baby on her back. She pointed. Along a mud track they found a shallow rivulet running through the long grass. The brothers stripped off their shirts and swept water over their heads. Alphonse produced his cake of soap. Emma hesitated, then moved upstream. She was filthy. She squeezed out her bra and pants and put them on again quickly, squelching her way back along the path. They waited for her, smoking thin cigarettes. Okay. Now breakfast. And then, to work.

Alphonse stood a few yards away from her, down the slope. Ten yards further on, one of the neighbours, and further down again, his son. And so on, as far as the cart where they were loading cabbage. A good crop, up here on this well-drained soil. Whup! Emma threw him another. Benito was cutting at the head of the line, throwing them one by one along the chain of men to the waiting cart. All men, except for Emma. She could throw pretty well, thought Alphonse. Without a household of her own to care for, why should she not do these things? And she wanted to; she was laughing. Pink as a piglet. Whup! Catch, turn, throw. Whup! Catch, turn, throw.

And I, he considered, am a rich man. I have empty pockets and a whole mountainside and clouds rolling at my feet.

The clouds grew darker and rolled right over their heads. At the first heavy drops of rain they ran back to shelter, breathless, soaked, spattered with mud, the thunder crackling in loops down the valleys. Rain rattled down all evening, all the night, all the following day. The weave of the roof let it in like a sieve.

The brothers prepared food, while in the corner an old lady sorted rice in a large, flat basket. Just out of reach of the bouncing raindrops, impressed by the volume of water hurtling past the eaves, Emma sat with her journal. '*You sit so silent here before the hills — not only quiet, silent; not to be disturbed. Scrape coconut, measure the rice, watch the fire; should I not watch you so closely? If I could just say something.*'

By the third morning the skies had cleared. The hills steamed as they shouldered their packs, heavy this time with cabbages and apples, things that could not grow in the wet heat of the valley. They passed a neighbouring farm, paying respects to Rosa's mother, and moved on, taking a different downwards path to avoid the mud in the river bed. Pampas grass streamed on the slopes, the coat of some great silver animal moving through the wind. The men set their pace, sliding and jumping down into the tree line through rustling miles of palm. When they reached a road at noon the sudden tarmac struck them as funny; they sat and ate oranges and laughed at the joke. A road! And on it, a truck, grinding along. Come on, English woman, now it is your turn. The driver will stop for you. We will ride back to Sibukay. Smile, then, and stick out your thumb.

She learned to wash in the river, and spread her clothes on a bush. To visit the market, to drink tuba, the coconut toddy, and walk reeling up the black hill at night. The fumbling for matches, the whush of a paraffin lamp. To live sticky with heat, to sleep uncovered, to eat rice for breakfast, lunch and supper.

On verandahs, or under the trees, she watched the sky clear and blue through the afternoons. Alphonse poring over his poetry book, Rafael dozing, the line of his chest, which had become so familiar to her, rising and falling. If there was singing in the village then they knew that it was Sunday.

The cockerels scratched and crowed; the ants ran along the walls.

He would take her back to Dumaguete. Straight away. Rafael would stay in Sibukay; there would be trouble for him in Dumaguete if Cita had reported him to the authorities. Sige na lang, let him stay here quietly until it blew over. All to the good. Ever since he, Alphonse, had seen Emma holding Rafael's shirt to her face, he had known that he must take her away at once.

In the half-light of evening he had come across her, standing still with her eyes closed, breathing into a shirt. She had dropped it at once when she heard him, casually dropped it from her hand. But he had seen.

Rafael said no goodbye, just sat in his usual place and watched them go. Emma sat with Alphonse on the bus in silence, a different silence; the trio was broken. Back through Oroquieta, swerving down the valleys and over the bridges to the harbour at Dipolog.

They waited for the boat in the heat of the day in the harbour café, with bottles of beer and time to kill. I will live in the present, Emma vowed. I will think of nothing else. Only what my eyes see and my ears hear, right now. Boats on the pale green water, men hauling on ropes, the steps where we landed weeks ago. Pigs squealing, those same men singing, sometimes beating time on an empty oil drum, women's voices behind walls, faintly a guitar playing no particular tune, and fainter, the invisible movement of water sounds.

I smell the beer, and a cigarette in Alphonse's hand, a flower in my pocket picked up from the ground in Sibukay, the salt smell of the harbour, of my own fingers under my chin. I feel – I just want to be within reach of *him*, not going away from him like this. But no, I must live in the present; I must think of nothing else.

Eight

Emma walked down the gangplank in Dumaguete, stood on the quay, and shrugged. It's all right, she told Alphonse; I can find my own way. The town was enormous, monstrous; pedicabs hooted, trucks chewed up the dust. The heat, after the cool of the boat trip, wrapped itself around her face as she trudged along the culvert to Valerie's house.

It was locked. She sat in a triangle of shade on the patio and scowled at the kids peeping through the fence. But she was quite good at waiting, now. Just sitting, with an empty mind. She had learned that.

Coming home later, Valerie was momentarily put out to find her there. Emma's room had been taken by a student from the college. No, Emma couldn't share with Valerie – her boyfriend was due to arrive soon. Emma said that she would sleep on the floor downstairs, it was fine, she was used to floors and there was heaps of room. Actually, said Valerie, there's Charles' room. Where's he gone? Oh, he's off again. Okay. Don't touch any of his stuff.

Back inside the concrete walls, she fell into a slump. She saw herself in a mirror for the first time in weeks. Her hair had gone reddish and slightly curly. But she stared into her own eyes and saw the same self as always.

Round and round inside the walls, round and round inside her head. To be within reach of Rafael, just within reach. It seemed mad that she had ever wanted to confess her feelings, now fearing that very thing: that he might guess. Probably he didn't think much of her. Probably she would have to give up everything for him, if he did. How could she ever approach him again, thinking such things? What did she want of him, anyway? Very little, and a lot, and again very little.

A poem might come out of the morass. She imagined pulling it up by the roots from the dark soil of her feelings. How painful it all was; she was bursting to express it.

Valerie was out most of the time, which was just as well. She was either at the college or on the beach with her boyfriend, as if nothing mattered – she didn't wrestle with her inner being, she was not a kindred spirit. There probably wasn't a kindred spirit in all the world. Thus it was, Emma knew, for some people. Camus wrote about it. The only person who had any grasp of such things at all was Alphonse, and clearly he wouldn't do.

It was stuffy in Charles' room. Downstairs, she worked on the poem, crossing out words, chopping up the lines, making fresh copies. *At charcoal fire, stir pan bare back, to lie too close, not close enough*. She had been sitting here, just like this, on the day when he suddenly appeared at the door. She looked up. He seemed to lean there, short and compact, supple as a cat. But there was nobody, just the light, glaring. *In doorways curve...*

She walked into town. Civilisation began like a tide-mark at Rico's, the narrow streets becoming a series of still photographs, wavering in the heat. She shopped unnecessarily, paying the prices that were marked, missing the market stall of Ozamiz, the friendly haggling, the scoops of this and that, wrapped in a twist of leaf. There were stalls by the roadside here but without Alphonse and Rafael she felt pinned into her foreign skin. Where was Alphonse, anyway? Doing whatever business it was that had brought him so suddenly back to Dumaguete. Doing a vanishing trick of his own.

His fingers followed the line. *Humankind cannot bear very much reality.* Well, there you are. T.S. Eliot. Alphonse closed the slim volume, allowing the words to reverberate within. He opened it again, re-tracing them. It all depended upon the reality, naturally. On the nature of reality, one could say. The concepts flowered in his head from the seeds of English which had been there since his schooldays.

Dawn points, and another day prepares for heat and silence. Out at sea the dawn wind wrinkles and slides. Exactly so. It did, precisely that. He went on eagerly, holding his breath. *The tolling bell measures time not our time, rung by the unhurried groundswell, a time older than the time of chronometers.*

It was all true. Never mind quite what; it was the truth. Charles had read the same passage months before, and shut the book decisively, laughing out loud. Then he had tossed it over. Take it, he said. He had tossed it over as if it was nothing, no more than a handful of paper he had found blowing along the street.

Alphonse listened to the music of the birds, the rhythm of the swaying trees. He had indulged somewhat in drinking over the past few nights. A little intemperance, a little madness now and then. After Mindanao he had taken one look at Dumaguete and headed for the hills. Here in a hut he had made with his own hands a few years before, he had a refuge where no one would disturb him.

His stomach gnawed; he had neglected to cook. A hangover had diverted him. Into the bubbling emptiness he had poured food for the intellect, for the soul. Words that he could lift from the page with his eyes. It was another kind of refuge. Now he must feed that other master, the body.

In the same province, on the other side of the river, Cita was also setting some rice in a pot to cook. She sang softly. Now it was okay. She had seen that foreign one with her own eyes, today.

First she saw Alphonse Romero yesterday walking along the track, and her heart went still. If he was back, then it was necessary to know about the woman. Because they had all gone at the same time on the *Victoriano* to Mindanao.

This she knew. It had been hard to do nothing. Loloy Romero had not said much to her, on the steps of the police station. It was better not to be seen in the town again, in case he should think of more questions to ask.

Her belly had been small and tight as a nut since then. Now it was sweet and full with relief. This morning she had walked with the baby past the path to the white people's house, to the crossroads and further, and seen that one with her own eyes, unmistakeable with the yellow toad hair. The woman was back, and Alphonse too, without Rafael. That meant that Rafael was free of the pink fingers and the purse full of foreign money.

She sprinkled a handful of sand over the fire, gazed for a moment at the sleeping child, and reached for the broom. Still singing, she tucked a slim arm across her back and began to sweep.

'I simply fail to understand how millions of years of natural selection could have programmed you to set your cap at Rafael, dear fellow though he is. It makes no obvious biological sense; it's an aberration.'

Charles sat at the table, marking specimens on a chart. He had arrived back just at the wrong moment, Emma thought. She had been confessing to Valerie, while they were lulled by the midday stupor, her tentative plan to go back to Mindanao by herself. She hadn't actually mentioned Rafael's name. Then Charles had blundered in, tall and sweaty, and put her on the defensive again.

'What do you mean: aberration?'

'Well, you're culturally incompatible, for a start. And if we get down to basics, the female of any species usually tends to pair with a larger, taller, more powerful male. It improves the gene pool. Surely you've noticed?'

Emma stared at him. 'Thanks a lot.'

'Dear girl, you will thank me. I know.'

'I'm not even listening.'

He shuffled through a sheaf of papers before looking up again. 'Do we have your mother's address?'

'What's she got to do with it?'

'Everything, probably. But that's by the by. On the practical side I thought we should have it, just in case you disappear into the jungle. But on second thoughts, don't bother. I'm bored with it. Let's go for a swim.'

He swung a towel over his shoulders and rammed a cap on his head. Valerie unpegged her own towel from the line. 'Coming, Em? Come on. No good scowling like that.'

I don't know these people, thought Emma as she tagged along behind. I don't belong with them. My heart is somewhere else. I must follow it. Dare I? I must, but I don't dare. It wasn't the journeying back to Sibukay alone that was daunting; she had no misgivings about that, now that she was an experienced traveller. It was more the thought of arriving.

In the evening the house was full of people. Students and friends from the town, Charles and Valerie's friends, not

Emma's. She was surrounded by strangers; the sense of it grew and grew. What were they talking about? World distribution, war, the communication of rats, the human dilemma. It was all nonsense.

She sat on the patio, listening to the hum of voices on one side and the hum of the bush on the other. A familiar figure appeared on the path – Alphonse, his red bag on his shoulder and his ready smile. The sight of him brought it all back in a rush, the mountains, the rivers, the cockerel crowing in the yard at Sibukay, Rafael, everything. She stood up and hugged him and immediately thought better of it, but it was too late. He squeezed her shoulder happily. He would join the others, he would thrive on their talk; he would be inspired.

Oh yes, Charles was saying, as he made room for them on the floor – did we tell you about the monster we found in Emma's room? She looked at him nervously; she was full of monsters. He ran upstairs, reappearing with a large lump, translucent as a jellyfish. Emma recognised it, it was the plastic coat she had brought from England, having read somewhere that it rained heavily in the Philippines. There were shouts of laughter. The plastic had melted and congealed in the heat, impossible to unfold. It was gross. She had brought that gross thing from the other side of the world, she knew nothing; she had to laugh about it with all these people.

Alphonse patted her arm. He wasn't laughing at her. She almost asked him outright – shall I go back to him, your brother, as I want to? Instead she kept a smile on her face, stretching out a hand absently to right an insect fallen on its back, watching it recover, clean its wings, fly away. *I'll go back to Mindanao*, she decided. *Tomorrow. I am afraid, but I know I will go.*

She awoke when the sun was already high enough to top the palm tree outside the window, and knew that she was too late for the boat. By the slant of the light through the jalousies she could tell that morning was well underway, gripping the concrete house on the edge of the town in its white-hot claw.

She had slept downstairs; she had done so since Charles reclaimed his room. He and Valerie were apparently still asleep, the student lodger too, unless he had slipped out before Emma woke. The beer she had drunk the night before had made her feel lonely; the sense of it sat on her like a great bag.

Maybe there had been no boat to Mindanao that morning, maybe they only ran on certain days. She must find out. She pulled herself up and quickly showered, glad of the touch of water in the dim shower house, with its mosquitoes suspended in the air. Ten minutes later, on the road to the harbour, her shoulders were heavy again with the heat and indecision, and the momentary cool was forgotten.

The man in the ticket office did not respond immediately to her question. She tried again. Ferry? Mindanao? Dipolog? Tomorrow? Er – ugma sa buntag sa Dipolog? He smiled at her in a way she did not entirely like, and shook his head. Today, he nodded. Tomorrow wala. He shook his head again and pointed to a notice board. Emma squinted up. Her head swam. This was not a good day. Nothing made sense; perhaps she was pre-menstrual. It was meant to be particularly awful to be pre-menstrual in the tropics, though she couldn't remember the previous month. Come on, she scolded herself, you know the days of the week perfectly well. Alphonse had made sure of that. There. There's a ferry on Saturdays, and that must be Tuesdays and Thursdays. She'd missed it that morning and she was stuck for two days. Salamaat, she said to the clerk. He was staring at her breasts.

The whole town was staring at her. Every quick, neat inhabitant watched her pulling herself back through the dust, a piece of alien matter heading for cover. She stopped at Rico's. The white sponginess of the bread would stuff up her longing, the sweet iron taste of Coke would give her a headache, and wipe away all hope for the rest of the day.

'You're moithering. That's what my mum always said when we moped about. Good word, isn't it? Not that I'm quite sure what it means. Could you go to the poste restante for me in the morning? Please. I've got a lecture at ten and a heap of marking to do.'

'Okay. Sorry, Val. I'm fine, really.'

'How's the writing coming along?'

'Pretty well. I'm in the middle of a poem right now, as a

matter of fact. Don't tell Charles.'

'You needn't bother about Charles. He's all right. Oh – shit.' The room was dropped into darkness as the electricity failed, the voice of Dylan vanishing from the tape machine. 'Oh, well. It won't come back now. I guess that's as good a reason as any to go to bed.'

Valerie lit a candle and went up the stairs. Emma heard her striking another match and presently the smell of a mosquito coil filtered down. The night was louder than ever now that the music had gone – it was deafening, a roaring sea. She wanted to sit forever, quite still, listening to whatever walked out there. But she must settle down and pretend to be asleep when Charles came in, flashing his torch around. He would kill her poem stone dead.

In the morning she awoke full of resolve. It would be all right. Her life was in her own hands; it meant nothing unless she took a few chances. Going back to Rafael was one of those chances.

He seemed so far away, not just in distance, but some other remote place, an unnavigable waterway. Know thyself, the ancient Greeks had said. It meant much more than that, of course. Emma just had to keep faith with herself for one more day and she would be as free as a bird, as true as an arrow.

She went obediently to the poste restante and found nothing for Valerie but, instead, a letter from her own mother. A whiff of England was released from the envelope as she tore it open. Bluebells and cheese, the cold moisture of a garden in the morning under a wall. *Make sure you keep something on your feet, darling. You can pick up all sorts of things in these places.*

She would be barefoot and free as a bird, right out along the curve of the earth. She crumpled the letter and let it drop, and the cold garden shrank back to a pinhole. Dumaguete ran a bright, hot tide over it. She stepped out onto the pavement, taking a different route away from Rico's. She'd be on that boat in the morning.

Nine

The town watched her go. She felt its gaze on her back as she crossed the gangplank; when the last line was thrown from the bollard she let out a sigh of relief. She'd slipped the net. As she looked along the shore, past the line of shacks where there was nothing but palm trees down to the water, she suddenly thought of the woman. She'd almost forgotten about her. It was gone, down into the past. A pebble on the seabed, a particle of sand.

The noise of the ship's engines filled her ears and she took a place amidships as Alphonse would have done. The engines were the heartbeat of an animal taking her away, a white horse over the sea. She was safe on its back; she was borne away. Carried away. Don't get carried away, people said. Oh, but she already was.

She was carried into the harbour at Dipolog, carried ashore on the crowded lifeboat in the late afternoon, across the hills and valleys on the bus. Darkness was sudden. It was dark when the bus shook into Oroquieta and everyone climbed down, when she came out of her trance and found herself alone.

There were lights, an open door, people seated at tables. She saw the bus driver. Faces turned towards her as she approached. Bus? Bus to Sibukay? There was a flurry of words and shaken heads. No one seemed to speak any English.

Suddenly she was very tired. She missed Alphonse. Somewhere out there, around the corner, was the house where they had stayed with the woman Marcelina and the men whose names she had never learned. A house on poles with wooden steps and a picket fence, a house from which she could hear the sea. But she didn't know which corner to turn, nor if she would know it in the dark — anyhow, she could hardly appear on the doorstep as if from another planet.

A woman pushed a tin cup of water into Emma's hand. Pagkaon? She enquired. What? Pagkaon, pagkaon, the woman insisted, lifting fingers to her mouth. Food. O-o, Emma replied. Men shifted to make room for her, seated around a single lamp. She glanced around at the shadows full of eyes and white teeth, grinning in the dark. A plate of rice was put before her. Beer? San Miguel? She shook her head. Tubig, salamaat. They chattered as she ate. Americana? No, English. Football? Prince Charles? O-o. There were some black bits in the rice which she couldn't see properly. The words came to her at the last minute. Busog na, salamaat. I'm full.

The driver and some of the passengers slept on the bus, their feet sticking out of the windows. She saw them as she picked her way carefully to a foul latrine. *Make sure you keep something on your feet, darling.* She herself slept on the landing of the stairs in the bus station, looking out at a huge yellow moon. Perhaps there would be a bus to Sibukay tomorrow, perhaps not. Perhaps there would never be a bus to Sibukay.

Before dawn the house was stirring. Men hawked into the dust, women appeared with sacks and bundles and trussed chickens. Emma hurriedly did up her bra under her clothes and brushed her hair. She found the woman who had fed her the night before and who now pointed urgently. Bus! Sibukay. Emma paid and thanked her, and climbed aboard. Her life was all like this now, up and down, round and round, sweating and drying and sweating and drying in the same clothes. She had had no breakfast. Hunger was something new and sharp.

The bus left her in the plaza near the market in Ozamiz, at the foot of the hill. She was nearly there. Doubt filled her lungs until she could hardly breathe. What could she say to him? *Oh, I thought I might as well come back – Sibukay is nicer than Dumaguete.* He would see straight through her, and turn away, and not want her.

She hesitated. It was nearly noon, not a good time for walking, not a good place to pause or to appear to be lost. She hailed a pedicab. Sibukay, o-o. Pointed uphill. Called out for him to stop outside Tatay's house and heard the pedicab putter away. There was no one about. She walked under the bo-ongon tree, up to the house, across the verandah, through the cool hallway and the kitchen and stopped at the back door.

They sat at the table. Nanay and Tatay and the neighbour's children and the houseboys and Rafael. He saw her and stood up, pushing back his chair. He said nothing. Then he fetched another plate, and indicated that she should sit.

'We go to market, we prepare food, chop, clean, chop. We see the sky blown open at sunrise. I fear what I knew that I would fear, that I will burden him. Just as his brother is better for a woman's company, so I feel him to be burdened. We light a first cigarette in the kitchen and go out into the dark with Eduardo and José, riding in the back of a truck to the beach. We swim. We lie under the trees, not speaking – I see a thin black snake by a rock and Rafael says: that one is poisonous. Nanay calls him a lonely man. Perhaps she means a loner. I realise the difference; there is a big difference.

Emma sat on the floor of the verandah. The boy swept the steps in front of her with slow, languid strokes. She wrote in tiny letters from the very top of the page; half her journal was filled already and paper was hard to find. The plenitude of things had fallen away – she was like a passenger stepping from a crowded train into an open land. The train had been going somewhere but now she had left it, and the points of reference had gone.

She finished her talcum powder. There was no basket in her room for rubbish, no tub or tin or bag in the kitchen.

In the entire house, no place to put rubbish, for there was no rubbish in this land. The stuff came from the market wrapped in leaves or paper, all burned or used again, every empty pot put to some other use. She stood in the hall, holding her little tin. It would not burn. If she buried it, a child or a dog would dig it up again. She had brought rubbish. She took it back upstairs and tucked it deep into her bag.

Rafael sat on the balcony of the neighbouring house across the path. She could look up and see him at any time. How many hours and days they sat, silent – it was a wonder. When he wasn't there she could not look for him, nor let herself think of where he might be; could never fall into step with him where people might see them together. In the eyes of the barrio she had been coupled with Alphonse. They asked: where is Alphonse? How odd it was, the friendship she felt for the one, and for the other this different and difficult pulling open of the heart.

He would not make any move towards her; she knew that.

Nanay sat at her sewing machine, her bare foot on the treadle. She pushed her hair back into its knot, and the wheel whirred around. The English one was out there, writing again in the book. Nanay shook her head so that more strands of hair escaped.

She would not eat good food; she would not eat pig. She came from a country where they had *electricidad*, she came to this poor place, and when a fine pig was killed she would not eat it.

The wheel whirred again. Nanay would at least make her a pretty dress, a simple terno; the English girl was nice and plump. A dress would compliment her shape better than shorts, which were not becoming on a young woman. Although she might not be so young, it was difficult to tell with white people. Father O'Brien now, he had had hair as white as an old man and a body as smooth as boy. Keeled over in the church one day, dead. Nanay crossed herself hastily and pushed back her hair.

On the balcony of the house across the path, Rafael Romero sat in his usual place, pulling at the ends of his moustache, thinking.

It was two days before Emma's twenty-third birthday when the telegram arrived. Addressed to her, care of Tatay, Sibukay, it was from Alphonse. *Extension of visa questionable needs your presence come immediately.*

She sat in the open space above the barrio on the slopes that had been proposed for a golf course and where carabao now lay in the mud holes like brown, living rocks. Beside her sat Eduardo and Bobo, Paulo and José, two of Vicente's sons, and Rafael. Rafael chewed on a piece of grass. They were mulling over her problem.

Her visa. She could stay in the Philippines for six months, but hadn't the travel agent in London said something about having to renew her permit after three months? She tried to think back into that distant, grey time. If that were the case then she had indeed overstayed that period by several weeks.

'How long have I been here?' she asked.

Since when? Since the first time, or this time? What day is it? They shrugged. Shall we make it Tuesday? Any objections to Tuesday, anyone? Tuesday, okay?

Don't worry, never mind the visa, they reassured her. Stay here. We will hide you. But she was worried. Must she go back now, to Manila, or even England — did she have to give it all up? Would the authorities decide her life for her? But she had already decided, she was already scraping away at that old life.

Rafael had not spoken. Then he said relax, relax. We will prepare pani-hapon. I will show you how to cook the heart of the banana; it is good.

Later, watching over the fire, he added, 'It may be a trick.'

Later still they gathered in Vicente's house, passing a guitar and a bottle of rum to each other in turn. No, I can't sing, she said. In my country we buy tickets to hear one person sing, someone who is a singer. Oh, but everyone can sing, they nodded — yes, you sing for us an English song. In a wavering voice she tried, to their laughter and applause. Another English song now, said Rafael. I sing it.

It may be tomorrow I'll find what I'm after
I'll throw out my sorrow, beg steal or borrow
my share of laughter

with you I could learn to
with you on a new day
but who can I turn to if you turn away?

She didn't try to catch his eye, but stared at the ground. He would not be looking at her.

She left again in the morning, heading for the bus to Oroquieta and Dipolog and the boat to Dumaguete. The sky was turning pink and Rafael busy cooking breakfast as she walked away.

In Dumaguete she went straight from the boat to Alphonse's yard. He heard her coming and stood up, smiling, his head on one side. She knew at once that there had been no problem with her visa, she could see it in his expression. He simply wanted her back. Sorry, he said, continuing to smile, pleased with himself.

Emma sat down. She dared not speak, struggling as she was with the impulse to hit him, to pick up a chair and break it on his head. Oh, you... you Filipino, she thought. Bloody cheek. What do you expect me to do – change my mind and stay here, then, since you bring me back, just so? You don't realise ... ah, but maybe you do.

He nuzzled up to her.

'Don't.'

'What is wrong?'

'Alphonse, there's a boat back to Mindanao the day after tomorrow. I'm going back. That's where I want to be.'

Charles looked up from his desk and made a face.

'Not you again.'

'Shut up.'

'Okay, okay. Let's start again. Hi there, Emma! Nice to see you. What's the state of play? Do tell. Or did you run out of Tampax?'

'Why do you have to be so crude?'

'Not crude at all. It's nature. They talk about menstruation quite freely here, have you noticed? My students are often late because of it. The females ones, anyway.'

'Where's Valerie?'

'Chez amour. Temporarily, I think. We've a staff meeting at five.' He peered at her. 'You look, er, a shade stressed. Little hiccup? Have a fag.'

'Thanks. Can I stay two more nights? No longer, honest.'

'By all means. Walay problema. Assuming you don't mind the floor. By the way...' he gathered up a pile of papers and waved them towards her. 'I thought of you when these came in. Take a look. Seems that American chap in San Carlos never did put in an appearance. You know the one you went to visit who never showed up? Dolores got the wind up and sent this on to me before she left the country.'

'She left?'

'Gone home. Finished her stint.'

'Oh. Right.'

'Her friend, this Ellis, was doing a little extra studying. Magbabarang – know anything about it?'

She shook her head.

'Thought not. Shamanism, that kind of thing. Around here they take it a step further than herbalism; a few do anyway. A mix of poisoning and voodoo, I gather. Powerful stuff.'

'What's it got to do with me?'

'Hang on, let me finish. There's so-called white sorcery, and black. Black sorcerers are magbabarang. Ellis was mixed up with it, either deliberately or by mistake. Guna-guna, it's called in Indonesia.'

'Oh, Indonesia now.'

'So? It's the same thing.'

'Well, I've never heard of it. I mean, not here.'

Charles blew out a thin stream of smoke. 'It's funny how these things work. Siquijor is known for it – regular gatherings up in the caves, according to this fellow.'

'I read all about the Philippines before I came out and there wasn't a word about it.'

'In your local library? I rather imagine not. You must dig a bit deeper. It's called research. Or you can be here as a tourist and never see a thing.'

'I see a hell of a lot more than *you* do; I'm *living* with Filipinos now. Not in a western house with all the comforts, not stuffing my head with ideas on paper. *American* ideas.'

'Stuff, stuff, stuff. Okay. I'm off. Duty calls. You know – work. The curse of the west. If only we could all be simple beings again, ah me. Make yourself at home. By the way, there's a bottle of Coke in the fridge, a western bottle of Coke, and it's mine, so hands off. Bye.'

Emma listened to the sound of his truck turning at the road before she wandered into the kitchen. In a paper bag she found some hard white buns, probably yesterday's. Tiny flies swarmed over the fruit basket. Pulling off a couple of small, pink bananas and chewing on a lump of bun, she opened the fridge. There was an open tin of condensed milk, Charles' bottle of Coke and a stack of cassettes. The fridge hummed indignantly as she pushed it shut. There was never any decent food in the house.

She stood at the desk, fingering the pile of paper. '*It is necessary to understand that these exchanges, as in all human (animal?) exchange, depend upon the participation of both parties. That is, the practice of ill-wishing (or well-wishing) produces clear results when the individual towards whom the intention is chan-nelled (the victim) is made aware of the intent.*' In the margin, the same hand had scrawled, much less neatly. 'Obviously.'

'*Therefore, where possible the victim will be notified of the intent. (By a sign, ie bones, feathers, eggs, stones, shells, fruit spilt to expose the seed, etc.) The significance of the signs, how and why they differ, is widely reported.*' Again, in the margin, 'But not proved?'

'*In cases where no sign is offered, ie in which the magbabarang is concealed from the victim for any number of reasons, the victim's spirit will be notified. Rituals ('haplit') involve dolls: in some cases, children. In other cases a likeness or symbol is drawn in the earth or sand and erased by hand or, especially, the tide.'*

The writing was as small and tidy as newspaper print, as if the writer had felt a shortage of paper. Emma rubbed her eyes. She couldn't take it in; she was tired. Also, she had just thought of something a lot more important. Now, after this business with the telegram, it would be clear to Rafael how she felt. When she went back to Sibukay again, he would know. She wouldn't have to declare herself. Everything would be all right – if, that is, he had any feelings for her.

She turned a few more pages. There were drawings of bugs, beetles and centipedes, not particularly nice. Towards the end of the report the unknown Ellis had written in a larger, less fastidious hand. *'The magbabarang are hired to avenge wrongs, the mananambals to heal sickness. The hex is said to transcend time and distance, even death. If not effective, the victim is presumed innocent. The power of the magbabarang is considered beyond question.'*

Tidying the papers back into a pile, she picked up a magazine and settled into the hammock. Her love just grew stronger; Alphonse had unwittingly smoothed the way. She could use this time for writing, but it was so hot; she could hardly think at all. Just beyond the fence the town seemed to shift a little in its dust, and settle closer.

Ten

Tatay watched the estranghero return to the barrio with some misgivings. So much coming and going, coming and going. Yet, the Americans were like that. They turned up as they pleased; he knew something of their ways. He sighed. His wife, whom he had never known to be mistaken in such matters, had seen the white girl look at Rafael Romero with love eyes.

Emma strode up the hill. It felt like coming home, home-coming to Sibukay. Every step was a relief. The last day with Valerie and Charles had been beastly and the journey back had given her too much time to think. What had Alphonse taught her, after all, by tricking her with a false telegram? English was for him a strange language, just as her behaviour was strange. His interest in western litera-ture was laid on top of his consciousness, not mixing with it all. She should hardly be surprised. His brother would be just the same. Wouldn't he?

Love transcended all that. She was drawn irrepressibly across the sea, jolted in the bus, waved on by the children, drawn she did not exactly know towards what. The Buddha exhorted his followers to let go of the Self, right? She could practically feel it happening, that letting go, as she turned off the road under the bo-ongon tree again and dropped her bag thankfully on the steps.

When Eduardo told him that the white girl had come back, Rafael shook his head slightly. So. He said nothing, however. The cockfight was just about to begin. He'd won twenty pesos on the last one and every cent he had was on the next.

Morning after morning she helped with coconuts. She came out as soon as she could, as soon as Nanay was satisfied that she'd eaten a good breakfast, even though she would not eat dried fish with her rice, and asked for eggs. Coping with Nanay at mealtimes had been a problem, with meat and fish literally pushed onto her plate. At last Emma said that it was against her religion, and this was understood. If it was against one's religion, what could one do?

Coming out into the cool morning air to where the men worked and taking up an iron bar, Emma squatted beside a pile of coconuts. One clean blow was needed to split them, but her attempts were messy and shattered the nut. Each piece was left upturned and drying in the sun. Everyone worked, the very youngest shooing the hens away. Carabao ambled by, pulling their carts between the trees, taking the husks to the charcoal pits, the copra down to the main road. The sun burned off the mist. She was happy; she was being useful or at least trying to be. She was working with her hands; this was real. She was learning the language. Magbuak ko lubi, she repeated to herself. I break open coconuts.

Happiness was strange stuff, though. Rafael kept his distance; he never came to sit with her as Alphonse had done, she was never alone with him. Taking his brother's place as her companion was obviously not right, not possible.

Sometimes the heartache was terrible, and not like happiness at all.

In the foothills behind Dumaguete, the old woman smoothed the fire's ash. So, the foreign one had slipped back to him. That was nothing. Yes, even though Cita had taken hair from her baby's head and clippings from the baby's nails and made a ring around the foreign house, still she had slipped away. There had been pebbles left at her gate and she had not seen them. She had not *seemed* to see them. But nothing was wasted.

The old one spat, holding up a hand as thin and fine as a twig to silence her granddaughter. Pshaw! If anything was a waste it was all this fussing, all this carrying on. It broke concentration, like this! She blew on the ash with a quick movement. It made clouds.

Keep an eye on the pebble at all times. Bitaw, it is there. No hurry. To hurry is to die.

Under the bo-ongon, on a rough stone seat, Emma sat after dark. The huge yellow fruits were underlit by the lamp on the verandah and hung overhead like strange moons. In another tree, swarming and circling, fireflies shone unsteadily. Paulo had once caught one in his cupped hands to show her. Aninipot. Daghan aninipot.

She sat cross-legged, hitching her feet under her knees, away from the mosquitoes. She had been just like all these insects lately, darting from place to place. Perhaps human beings were the same; perhaps it was just as pointless to be always on the move, and just as difficult to stop. She herself found it hard to stop, to be patient, to let the days tick by. Rafael apparently found it easy.

She gazed into the darkness. From the direction of Vicente's house came the click of mah-jong tiles; sometimes laughter. Nanay would soon appear at the top of the steps, wringing her hands in agitation and calling her in. Come, come, come. There were spirits in the night and Emma must not sit out there alone. Night after night Emma obeyed meekly, reluctantly. But just then she heard voices from the hills behind, shouts, and the sound of running feet. She stared out fearfully. A figure hurried past, then a second, then a group of people, carrying something. There were cries and groans. A light flared further down, and another. She kept very still.

The voices at Vicente's were raised. She left her seat and ran to the steps, just as Pablo the houseboy slipped past her. She heard him speak to Tatay urgently, she heard Nanay give a swooping, keening cry. They had no time for her. She went to her room and pushed the jalousies wide.

The cockerels crowed, as usual, up and down the barrio, long before dawn. Emma dressed quickly and went outside to the water butt, dipped the enamel jug and splashed her face. There were voices in the kitchen. Nanay, at work with her hair still in a loose knot hanging down her back, lifted her arms when she saw Emma and broke into a long, excited stream of words accompanied by much head shaking. Emma shook her own. She had no idea what was going on.

She stood uncertainly on the verandah. All seemed as usual. The hens rustled about in the leaves. Wisps of cloud hung over the trees like smoke, as they did every morning. She glanced up. On the balcony of the house across the path there had been a movement. Rafael had seen her, perhaps had waited to see her. Sure enough he came now between the trees, scattering the hens. Her heart squeezed painfully.

'Buntag. Kumasta?'

'Buntag. Yes, okay. What's going on? What's the matter?'

'You hear also? Last night, na lang? It is Toni. Brother of José and Paulo, also. A knife, yes? Here, and here.' He stabbed at his own chest.

'Is it bad?'

'Bad? O-o, he is dead.'

'Christ.' She looked past him towards Vicente's house. The mist was lifting gently, the smell of breakfast came from the kitchen behind her. 'What happened?'

He shrugged. 'Bandito. Up there.'

'What about the police? Or the army?'

He laughed shortly. 'Bandito, the army, the same. Army rebels. Is possible. MNLF, maybe.' She looked puzzled. 'Liberation Front. Who knows? Sagdi...' he added, changing his tone. 'Is okay. You don't worry.' He cleared his throat, then with a slight movement indicated that she should follow him through the house.

Breakfast was ready on the long table by the back door. Tatay emerged from his room in his vest, a towel around his neck. The boys were setting down saucers of fish, vinegar, steaming white pyramids of rice. Tatay said a loud and rapid grace, and spoons and fingers dug into the food. She looked around for the right moment to speak, to offer her sympathy. Rafael ate steadily. She said nothing. When he finished he drank a glass of water in one draught and left the table. I never know what to say, she thought. I never know what to do.

She found him afterwards sitting by the side of the road alone, waiting for her.

'We go to the fish pans.'

'Now?'

'O-o, now. Okay?'

Today we walked down the hill for the first time together, with no one else. In a carabao cart, lurching and rolling through the trees. Bright red dragonflies. The wake at Vicente's tonight, everyone singing, drinking, playing cards. Sitting in the yard. Kapoy-ikaw? he asks. Yes, I am tired. He walks me home, disappears. Whistles before sunrise under my window. Down the hill again in the dark, this time with Eduardo and José but something has changed. I am with Rafael; it is like that. We climb another hill, up and up, a chapel at the top with bells. Kaadlawon, dawn over Ozamiz, over the sea.

She was writing very small, starting at the very top of each page and covering, without paragraphs, every inch. The notebook of her journal was half-filled, the spine of it broken, the corners worn inwards. She had the journal and her passport: nothing else of any importance now.

Rafael sat with her on the verandah. Sometimes in the siesta hour he would appear, sometimes not, sitting a little distance away and busy with his mending. He mended his own clothes, and the clothes of the children, using a big needle and a thick thread. He never asked about her writing and never tried to look at it.

She borrowed a needle from Nanay and joined him, making a new pocket for her jeans. They had not spoken for a while. She glanced over at his sleeveless shirt, his bare arms; his scarred face with its black moustache, bent over his work. What had Valerie said? *You bet he'd be interested – you're foreign, aren't you?* She had a knot in her thread. He looked up, enquiringly. Painstakingly she tried to loosen it then dropped her work to her lap.

'I need a wife,' she sighed.

He hesitated for a fraction, then slapped his knee and laughed. She blushed. The thick, hot air held onto her words.

'Maybe we could leave.' There. She had said it.

'Kuan? Mobiya? Leave? Go? To Dumaguete?'

She lifted her shoulders. 'You said – didn't you talk, you and Alphonse, about leaving?'

'Leave, na lang? Go out? Back door?'

'Maybe. Or the other way. From Manila. Front door.'

He stared at her. Then broke off a length of thread and held up the needle.

'Sige. We think about it.'

Eleven

It was at siesta time when the rains came again. Emptied from the sky as if from a bucket. Pablo hurriedly unhooked the paraffin lamps that hung outside, the one over the table by the kitchen door and the one over the steps, and took them in.

Palm branches were carried down the hill in sudden, muddy torrents. Water poured from the edge of the water butt, thunder rippled this way and that. Emma did a little dance; it was so exciting, she had to be out in it. The rain hammered down on her head and bounced off the path at her feet. She couldn't be wetter, she was soaked but she was cool. The cool was like an antidote to an enchantment after all the sticky heat.

She expected to hear Nanay's voice at her back, but none came. The road was deserted, a furious river hurtling past where the coconuts had lain a few days before.

Moments later a woman in a doorway called to her husband. Called again, above the din of the rain on their roof. See — look there. The Americana standing under the banana tree, out in the storm, with her eyes closed. Leaning her cheek against the tree... 'sus! that is a strange one. Her husband looked at the woman in the wet clothes under his bananas, and agreed.

Emma stayed out in the rain until her fingers went crinkly. The newest mosquito bites on her feet took on a soggy, uncooked appearance — that was a bad sign. She would have to get dry. On her way back to Tatay's she saw Rafael on the balcony and waved.

'This like England, no?' he called.

She let Nanay scold and bustle her inside. She must take off her wet things and then try on the new dress Nanay had just finished making — yes, yes, now. Alone in her room she rubbed her hair dry and pulled the pale, turquoise material over her head. There was no mirror. No mirror or glass anywhere in the house.

She sat on the edge of her bed. It was almost as dark as night, with the heavy clouds and the jalousies half closed. She looked down, at her breasts flattened sideways and her pink knees sticking out like ghostly marshmallows below the hem. A big girl in a green dress with puff sleeves which she would as soon die as wear in public.

A little moan escaped from her mouth and she clamped it shut. The wooden partitions stopped short of all the ceilings; there was no privacy and no chance to cry. She had recalled with shame how she had dared to ask Rafael to leave the country with her — he had been polite, but not mentioned it since, had said nothing, but vanished again for three days and then returned as if nothing was happening. As indeed, it was not.

There was a cough. Emma composed her face and opened the door to Nanay, who exclaimed at the sight of her, chirruping to herself as she did so. Certainly the wings of a butterfly sat rather differently on such a figure, which was solid even though the girl did not eat pig. Perhaps the dress could be altered a little. She said so, but the girl didn't understand. She indicated pulling a garment over her head, nodding. Okay, okay na lang.

Outside, the rain had stopped, except for water dripping from a thousand leaves. The road steamed. Emma watched Nanay's retreating back in the dim passage, crushed by the sense of being far away, impossibly far.

The smell of wet jungle clung to the walls all that night. Midnight was as hot and thick as her father's greenhouse in her childhood in July. Emma dreamed of brown roots crawling through the soil, poking their fingers into her, turning her to compost.

In the morning every plant had grown by several inches. The banana in the yard seemed many feet taller and ready to unfurl new deep green, triumphant leaves. Pausing on the steps, she heard cell division in deadly earnest on all sides. Also, the sound of a pedicab puttering up the hill. Carlos, the driver, had an envelope between his teeth and a chicken swinging from the handlebars. He swung the machine around with a flourish and grinned at her.

'Emma Clarke, Emma Clarke!' he cried, holding the letter aloft in one hand and the chicken in the other. 'For you!'

Not another telegram, please, let it not be another telegram, she thought. Who else knows I'm here? 'Oh, it's from Charles.' She recognised the writing. 'Thanks, Carlos. Salamaat. And, no thank you. No chicken. Walay manok, salamaat-a?'

'Yes, yes. Manok, good. Fet. Fat, no?'

'Hang on a minute.'

She ran for Nanay, and then left her with Carlos and the chicken, retreating to the verandah with her letter. There were two envelopes inside the first, one from her mother and one from her friend in London, both folded with a note from Charles.

Hail, great white queen. The enclosed were waiting at the poste restante. All is well back here in the world. We have an addition to the household, a puppy called Ginamos. The Winter's Tale forges ahead; Alphonse has joined the drama group. Val sends regards etc etc − Charles.

'Dear Em. Guess what. You know that Kevin from deliveries well we're going out now. He's got a Fiesta and you know he's football mad so there I am freezing at matches every Sat. He's really nice and his mum is. I phoned your mum for your address. Everything's the same at work only Jan's got my locker now and I got yours. I'll have a holiday too when I've saved up. By the

way there's a sale at Edgars, I got a coat...'

She sat on the steps and closed her eyes. The voices behind the trees and the swish of Pablo's brush came to her ears. Then she opened the second letter.

'Darling Emmie. What a relief to hear from you at last. Nearly a month since your first letter but there was no date on this one; maybe it was held up somewhere. We're so glad to hear you're having a lovely trip. Your new friends do sound nice. You don't actually say what they teach. How big is the college...?'

The bits of paper from England choked her. She fetched her own paper and a pen; she must write back at once and tell them. This was no holiday, this was Life.

She chewed the end of the pen until ink leaked out of it in blobs. She imagined standing on her parents' doorstep with Rafael, tried to place his figure, with the bandy legs in trousers instead of shorts, the woolly hat, the bloodshot eyes – she imagined him in the grey porch between the pebble-dash walls. She saw her mother's bedding plants edging the gravel drive. How would he stand the cold? Not just the winters, but the cold of Englishness? The image slid away. Instead, there he was, heading towards her, warm, real, in colour.

'Buntag, Rafael.'

'Buntag. Kumusta?'

'Okay na lang.'

He looked serious. 'Carlos come. From Cadre. His cousin's son is dead. Is tipus.'

'Typhoid?'

'O-o. I go now. Don't write it.' He added, seeing her paper. 'Don't write it to your home.'

She nodded.

'Sige.' He turned to go. 'Yes? Something you want?'

She wanted him closer. He kept that space between them, holding himself away. But she hadn't spoken. She shook her head.

'I've met someone I like very much.' She crossed it out. *'One member of the family I told you about is called Rafael. Rafael Romero. Rafael Romero. Rafael Romero.'* She wrote urgently, angrily, to herself, crossing out the words as she did so. *Typhoid. Stabbing. Death. Life. Hot black mountain sky smell water man gihigugma ko ikaw Rafael Romero*

Nanay, returning from the yard with the now dead chicken, knew that her guest was crying by the way her shoulders moved up and down. She crossed herself. That one would not even eat chicken, not fish, nothing. Only egg and calabasa. And look what happened.

She couldn't worry about it; there was work to be done. Her husband would be sixty tomorrow and one chicken was just a beginning.

Tatay looked around the hall in satisfaction. Dasok! It was crammed with people. The whole barrio was there under his roof, his children and their children, his nephews and nieces and he couldn't quite see who else at the back. So! Who next to sing? Paulo? Good. They'll hear him all the way to Ozamiz. Where's the guitar?

Unable to wait, Tatay launched into loud song himself, helped along by loud applause. He saw that his guest, her face round as a butong in the lamplight, was being rather quiet. Hey! Hey you! I love America! She smiled and shook her head, saying something. Yes! he insisted. General MacArthur! I remember! The language came rushing back to him. You – America, you far from... kuan? From home. From mother and father. You – gihidlawon? Home*sick*? You – my daughter!

Thunderous applause filled the room. He slapped his thigh. There. She was his daughter now; they were all liberated by the Americans. Paulo! Paulo! Music! Drink!

Rafael passed a bottle of rum to Emma.

'Filipinas don't drink rum, do they?' she asked in surprise.

He shrugged. 'You are Filipina? No! So.'

She sipped from the bottle. Perhaps the question of drinking was something she should raise with him. 'You like to drink?'

'Why not?' He leaned forward a little. 'We go to Manila? You want it?'

She nearly reached out, touched him. No, not yet. 'Yes. We go out?'

'First, Manila. We drink to it, no?'

'Is there any tuba?'

'Maginom kamig tuba.'

He disappeared. Behind her knees, the sweat was running, not just because of the heat but the great sun of happiness rising over her life. He came back with two glasses and clinked his own against hers. The palm toddy was an acquired taste, definitely, but she was acquiring it. Before she had finished the glass her head seemed to swim upwards with a curious, curving movement.

Nanay saw the clink of glasses and clucked her tongue. Daan pa ako, just as I thought. And after her husband's speech, too, which she had been unable to follow but which had clearly concerned their guest. Well, he was enjoying his birthday. She must keep an eye out for Pablo, and make sure he was around to help the old man to bed.

Twelve

'We will need paper, no?'

'Yes.'

'You have papers. I have none. Basiyo.' Rafael spread his hands over his pockets as if to reveal their emptiness. 'I ask Vicente. He ask cousin in Ozamiz.' He frowned. 'Police clearance. Foo! Registration of birth. Photo, signed by barrio captain. Police clearance. Ay, ay, ay.'

'Is there a problem?'

He considered. 'Many problem, bitaw. But we try. It need money. All this.'

'Well, I have money.'

He looked at her curiously and then at the ground. They sat, as usual, by the road, on the white-painted stones that marked the path for those walking at night between Tatay's and Vicente's. She felt a pang of alarm. All she had left was in traveller's cheques, a few hundred pounds, not much, but a hundred per cent more than he had. The scales were loaded badly right from the start.

She thought of him disappearing to the cockfights, the way he would gamble and drink when he had the chance.

'I may have enough; I'm not sure,' she said slowly. 'I can pay for you but... can you promise not to waste it?'

He remained very still. 'I make no promise,' he replied, at last.

Of course. Of course, of course! How stupid she was, how crass. She could make no bargains; she would choose to be with him and take the consequences. They were free spirits in the great cosmos. Money only happened to be hers because she came from a world of payment and papers and all that stuff. She despised it. She'd nearly fallen into the trap of ownership which made people fearful, greedy. He had corrected her with his brief, honest reply. She was humbled.

'I'll need to go to the bank in Ozamiz.'

'Sige. Palungsod kami. We get photo, also. Ugma sa buntag, okay?'

They took a lift into the town on the back of a truck. Rafael led her through wide, sun-slanted streets, picking his way between the pavement stalls. I'll follow him anywhere, she thought. The market gave way to a few glass-windowed and deserted shops, their blue-eyed mannequins standing stiffly in the dust, dressed in ballgowns. For you? he teased. In the bank Emma changed a cheque while he waited outside, and in a dark booth they took turns to sit under a photographer's flash bulb. The results would be ready in two days.

They sat in the plaza in the midday heat, eating mangoes in the shade of some thick-leafed tree. Init karon, she said. He nodded. The language was like a magic formula, to utter sounds and to be understood. He had learned his English with Alphonse, he told her, in the American air base of Angeles near Manila. At school also, he added.

She would also learn the language of his silence. He lay down on the parched grass, unknotting the kerchief from around his neck and spreading it over his eyes. Almost instantly his breathing became light and regular.

She searched in her shoulder bag for her journal. The ability to lie down anywhere and sleep for an hour was a gift she didn't have, even if it was so hot that the air quivered on the ground. It was the best time for her to write, when nobody was about to pester her with questions. The only other time she was ever alone was at night, and then it was dark.

How funny it was to think of having electricity again, and carpets, hot water, telephones – what weird, crazy things people had! She was finished with all that. She and Rafael might travel and see the world, take a look at England and the way of life she had once known, and then come back to the Philippines and live simply. Up in the mountains maybe, where it was a bit cooler.

She gazed at him, at his beautiful, strong body relaxed and asleep only feet away, the shirt worn thin and soft, frayed at the neck, the brown skin of his arms where veins crossed the muscles, down to his hands. There were no words to describe the way that her whole life was invested there, in that figure. She made an attempt to sketch him but it was no good; she couldn't capture it.

After an hour he stirred, sat up and shook himself. Squinting across the plaza he indicated a pump in the far corner, and she rose obediently. They drew water for each other, splashing their faces, their heads, the back of their necks. Drank. He set off without a word towards the road out of town.

'Hey, hey, hey!' It was Carlos on his pedicab, streamers flying from the handlebars, skidding to a halt beside them. Rafael spoke and gestured for a while over the noise of the engine, and then beckoned to Emma. She climbed into the tiny seat while he sat behind Carlos, who revved the engine with a few exaggerated turns. They roared away, Emma clutching the hot metal bar happily. In ten minutes they screeched along a track that rapidly became sand, where a few huts stood high on their wooden poles and the sea lay flat and brilliant on either side.

She shook the grit from her hair. Rafael and Carlos were surrounded by a group of men, all talking at once and slapping each other on the back. She smiled into their unintelligible talk, not trying to decipher it. She was looking at the sea and its circular plate, white at her feet, shining through greens and purples into dark pewter patches. It glared up at the sky. Not a rock to be seen, not a cloud. She shielded her eyes.

In the shade of small boats drawn up on the sand a group sat watching a game of chess. Rafael greeted them, accepting a cigarette, which he offered to Emma. They would share it. Money was slapped down as the game progressed and someone shouted to Rafael. He hesitated on the edge of the circle. Then he went back to Emma and took the last of the cigarette from her hand.

'Maglangoy lang kita. Let's just swim, no?'

She left her bag by a boat, with some misgivings about the money inside. But that was unworthy. She took off her sandals. He had stripped off his shirt and stood, waist-deep, looking out at the horizon. As she waded in, in her clothes, he dived. He didn't surface for a long time and when he did, it was some distance away. This is how we travelled, she thought, in the same bus, but not together. Now we swim at the same time, but separate. The significance of it made her draw breath sharply. Why did people glue themselves together – whatever for? There was enough space, plenty for everyone. She kicked out, swimming.

Half a mile from the spit of sand the water became shallow again. Just as she realised that she would never get cold in such water and could play in it forever, a boat skimmed towards her. It was Carlos in a canoe, grinning. Rafael appeared on the other side, holding it steady; she must climb in, come on! He pointed to where the surface of the sea ruffled and chipped in the distance.

'Isda. Fish. See, the sakayan. They come.'

He looked over his shoulder at the shore. She followed

his look to where the boats from the sand were now in the water and heading towards them. They were going to fish. She couldn't watch.

But Carlos turned the canoe, rocking it and tipping them over. They swam ashore and sat on the beach while their clothes dried. Out on the sea where they had been the sakayan hovered, vulture-like, over a single spot. So much death, so much life. Emma saw that her own skin was almost as brown as theirs, the hairs gold.

Dark fell as they rode back to Sibukay. Rafael, a large fish over his shoulder, bid her 'gabii' briefly and was gone. She entered Tatay's house like a truant, with the beginnings of a headache.

Two days later she felt Nanay watching her with a look of disquiet and reproof. She had not seen Rafael since he had said that he would 'make plans', and she had given him two hundred pesos.

She sat in the yard by Rosa's house, away from Nanay's gaze, her legs astride a bench, scraping coconut. The grater had been hammered into the bench like a jagged old bottle opener. Perhaps it was an old bottle opener. What did they call it? A kudkuran, kagoran; something like that. So many of the words sounded the same and she was shy of using them now, without Alphonse to correct her patiently.

She twisted the coconut this way and that, as he had done up in Gala. She had not thought of Alphonse all this time; she would not think of him now. Shavings fell from the nut into the bowl below, but it was hard work. She wasn't holding it right, as he had done. But no, she mustn't think of him.

Rosa stirred something in a pot over the fire. Binignit, she said, pointing to the mixture. Emma squeezed water through the coconut scrapings and indicated that she would mix it in. Rosa nodded. They were getting along fine; it looked delicious. Now, in England, they would stop and have a cup of tea. Or coffee. Here it was water, water, water. Great jars of tuba sat on the shelf, bubbles glupping to the surface. There was no tuba in England. What would Rafael make of it all? What would he do? What about Alphonse?

There was another question. At that moment a child wriggled into Rosa's lap and a ball of coconut was pressed into his mouth. It was difficult to see whose child belonged to whom; the kids ran freely between one household and the next; fed, washed, carried and loved by everyone. Rafael often took a tub of washing to the pools and spent the morning soaping and rinsing children's clothes. Did he miss his own children? That was the question she had once asked Alphonse. He misses them, he had nodded.

She looked at the yard – the earth, packed down hard and smooth as stone and meticulously swept, the bench, the basketball hoop, the smoke of the fires, the canopy of trees. Paradise. Meanwhile she hoped and planned for other things; it was like a sickness she had.

That night, fumbling about in the dark washhouse with the roar of the cicada in her ears and dipping a bucket in the water drum Pablo left every day in the dry bath, she decided to give up the hopes and plans. She wanted to attach herself to Rafael too much. The Buddha was right; she must relinquish it.

She put her toothbrush into her mouth and then spat violently. It was alive with ants. Ugh. She spat and spat. Paradise was difficult, and it was hot.

Morning in Sibukay. I dream of another place and when I wake up, I should be gone from here. A guest cannot stay forever. There are a hundred reasons to begin my travelling again. It would take more courage to stay than to go. I don't know if I am brave enough. I am alone. I AM ALONE.

I can't stay here without you; you are the reason. Do you belong here? Tell me. Will I make you unhappy? I should be happy and not afraid. I wish I knew what you were thinking. I hardly know you at all. Never mind that. I won't let you down, I'm sure of that anyway. That, and the morning, the evening, the mountains, trees, silent days – yet I am stifled and crammed inside.

To be alone and not to be alone are both unbearable. Not to be alone, that is the worst one. What I mean is, it's hard to trust him. I hear the word 'bulangon' and think: cockfight. He's got my money, he'll gamble my money away – and what if he does? And now that I've given him money doesn't it change things between us? It's all up to me and I don't want it to be so. You can't be indebted to me so consider it yours. As you will.

*How can I sit quietly, while you go, and I don't know where –
but I can't be assertive. If we leave together then it announces that
we have a romance, which isn't true so let's stay apart, yes I agree.
We may never leave! We may spend all my money and go our
separate ways and probably will. Perhaps I should just fly away
and leave you free, maybe you want that. Your ability to silence is
your best gift and also the worst. Only I dread that you might be
nice to me because – damn it! NOT ANOTHER WORD.*

She hid the journal when Nanay called her to lunch.
Sitting down to her plate of rice she named, to Nanay's
satisfaction, the dishes on the table. Onion, sibuyas.
Tomatoes, tamatis. String beans, batong. Cabbage, repolyo.
Her fingers hovered over a saucer. Isda? Nanay nodded.
Kinilaw? No. Ginamos. Ginamos? O-o. Funny, that was the
name of Charles and Valerie's puppy, surely.

Lying on her bed for siesta was not so much to sleep as
to shut out her thoughts. She pushed the jalousies wide
and lay in the stripes of light, covering her legs with the
green terno against mosquitoes. Her mind was blank. She
lay quite still, even when the village stirred again in the
mid-afternoon, until she heard a familiar whistle under the
window. He was there; he had come back from wherever
he had been. She jumped up quickly, trembling.

He squatted on the steps, calm and still. He held out an
envelope. Inside were their photographs in thin, paper
frames. His face looked like a 'wanted' notice for a hill

bandit, the conjunctiva spread wing-like across one eye. Hers had a slightly frightened expression, her shoulders hugely filling the bottom of the frame.

'Beauty and the beast,' he said, unexpectedly.

'Oh.' She looked at them again and put them back into the envelope. 'Shall I keep them with my passport?'

'O-o. You keep. And this.'

He handed her money, a fold of notes. There was a moment's silence. 'Musukad kita dinhi.'

'Say it again?'

'We start from here. Tomorrow, we go. Sige, ha?'

'Oh. Yes. Good.'

Yes. Good. Good that she was keeping her reactions in check. Take a deep breath, she told herself. That's it. Relax. The money in her hand was as worn and soft as fine cloth. He hadn't wasted it. She wouldn't count it. Not yet. Maybe not even later. A sudden thought ruffled her.

'What about Nanay and Tatay? What will I say to them?'

He considered. 'Is okay. I explain it. I make it: small-small.'

In the morning she walked past the seat under the bo-ongon tree with a sense of sadness. She had sat out there for hours the night before and for once Nanay had not called her in for fear of the spirits. She might never see fireflies again, might never live in another paradise, could hardly remember why it had ever seemed less than perfect. The darkness had been so dense, filled with the chink of mah-jong, the voices and the rustlings – and now it was all over and there was no time to stop.

Emma guessed that Rafael hadn't announced their plan the day before, but now everyone gathered in consternation. Eduardo, Paulo and José, Rosa, the children, Nanay and Tatay. Rafael lifted Rosa's hands to his forehead, and turned to Emma.

'She say, Vicente is in the town. He leave early. He would say goodbye also.'

Emma nodded. She shook Nanay's hand and pressed her arm inadequately, thanking her for the dress, for everything. Nanay pushed her hair back into its coil. Rafael lifted her hand and then Tatay's. As Emma climbed into the pedicab with her bag on her lap and Rafael swung into the pillion seat, Tatay bellowed something above the noise of the engine.

'Makahinumdum ka namo!'

Thirteen

'What did he say?'

'Who say?'

'Tatay. As we were leaving – he shouted something.'

'Makahinumdum ka namo. You'll remember us. He say it to you.'

They sat on the steps of the pier. The ferry was expected in an hour, or two, or three. Dipolog lay quietly, as before, the hills on the opposite side of the bay edged with green, the fishing boats, the basnig, lying like birds at anchor and rocking gently on their delicate struts. Emma sketched them, on the inside cover of her journal. She hardly liked to write anything with Rafael nearby; the sketch would be enough.

'Americana?'

A well-dressed Filipino was looking over her shoulder.

'No, English.'

'Ah. English.' He grinned. 'You wait for the boat also? You want a beer?'

Rafael came closer, speaking a few words to the stranger, whose expression flickered before he extended the invitation. Rafael turned to her. 'We go for a beer, no?'

They sat in the bar where she had waited with Alphonse; this time with the stranger who said that he had been to America many, many times. He was a little drunk, and had with him a crowd of friends who appeared with the next bottles of San Miguel. Rafael drank one down, and accepted another. Emma toyed with her own. She couldn't see the harbour from her seat; she wanted to watch for the ferry.

The party around the table grew noisier. The stranger stood up and made a speech and Rafael did the same, turning out his pockets. See! My clothes are all I have. They cheered enthusiastically. Bottles were crashed together and beer sprayed over them all. At last another customer leaned out of the window and gave them a shout. The ferry was coming in.

In the crush at the gangplank she looked at Rafael anxiously. Please let him not be drunk. Sagdi, he reassured her. They will sleep. He led her away from the ship's bar and up to the main deck, finding a space and immediately falling asleep himself.

She stared down at the sea. This was the sixth time she had taken the ferry. The breeze blew cool and salty on her cheeks. A young man in a crisp white shirt tapped her on the arm. 'Excuse. The captain say, you come to the bridge, please?' She frowned. Rafael opened his eyes. 'Sige. I look after your bag.'

She followed the young man across the ship. On the bridge stood three men, one at the wheel, one the captain and one a white man with a clerical collar. The captain beamed, introducing them like long-lost relations. Would she like a drink? Coca Cola? A little whiskey? The man asked a few polite questions. What was she doing in the Philippines? Was she travelling alone? Why? Oh lord, she thought. I came here to get away from this.

She excused herself as soon as politely possible. *This is the very thing that divides me from everyone else. Here I am, coming out of this door marked 'private', having been picked out of all the passengers to have drinks with the captain and the only other white-skinned person on board....* She slipped back to her place, where she really belonged, with Rafael. He read her face and laughed, making the calming gesture with his hand. She shivered suddenly. *I can look at him now and think: he will be mine.* But it was a crazy thought. He had never touched her.

Dumaguete, visible on the horizon in the late afternoon, produced in him a fixed watchfulness. He gave the approaching coast his steady attention until Emma found herself also scanning the beaches and the trees. Empty, they seemed to be awaiting something. She backed away from the rail uneasily. Just before they docked he spoke to her quietly. She would go straight to Charles and Valerie and stay there. He himself had to go (he waved his hands towards the other side of the town) and make arrangements. Urong sa balay, stay in the house. He would call for her later, and she was to be ready.

He slipped into the crowd, leaving her with her bag. Her legs suddenly felt weak. So they were leaving almost at once and not staying here at all, no more time in the English house with Charles and Valerie but a quick turn around and then goodbye. The crowds on the wharf streamed around her. She must not stand still. She must walk.

The stores were opening again after their afternoon sleep. She caught sight of herself in the glass window of Rico's, a stranger walking on a screen, insubstantial as the fear gnawing at her back. She crossed the culvert almost at a run, scattering hens, head down along the single track to the concrete house.

Valerie, discovering her waiting again on the patio half an hour later, did not seem overwhelmingly pleased. Perhaps Emma imagined it; she herself had changed a lot lately, she had lived in Sibukay for so many weeks and now she was a woman in love, with immediate and exciting plans. She hesitated to mention the plans straight away, but accepted some tea.

'This is divine. I never thought tea would taste so good.'

'It's only Black Cat and condensed milk.'

'They don't drink tea at all in Sibukay.'

'Oh, right.'

'Where's the puppy? Charles said...'

'The kids ate him.'

'Christ.'

Emma was silent, and then, as though remembering something, added, 'I'm not actually staying at all this time. I mean, you don't need to worry about where I'll sleep or anything. And thanks, anyway – for letting me stay so often, I mean. But we're moving on tonight. I just came to say goodbye, really.'

'Who's "we"?'

'Me and Rafael.'

'Ah, you got him, did you?'

'Not at all. It's just time to move on, that's all, and he wants to come with me.'

'I bet. Well! Charles will...'

'It's none of his business.'

'Soon see. Here he comes now.'

A truck door slammed in the clearing between the trees and a moment later Charles appeared on the patio, his arms piled high with books and bananas, a large papaya balanced on the top.

'Aha. The adventuress returns once more.'

Valerie raised her eyebrows in Emma's direction.

'Hi, Charles. Kumusta?'

'Maayo man.' He looked from one to the other. 'Am I interrupting anything?'

'Oh, I was just telling Val that I'm not staying.'

'She's moving on. With Rafael.'

'Moving on where to?'

'We're going up to Manila. He wants to come back to England.'

Charles deposited the books on the desk and stacked the fruit in the bowl. Crossing the room, he sat down beside Emma and looked very intently into her face.

'No, don't wriggle off. I need to get this straight. You and Rafael have teamed up and you're going to Manila, right? He doesn't have a passport, right? How's...'

He grabbed her wrists as she tried to put her hands over her ears. 'No. Listen to me. You can't do this. Listen to me.' He dropped his voice. 'Emma! You have to listen. Where's the money coming from?'

'I've got some. I'll send for some. Get off me!' She lunged away and he tightened his grip.

'You won't make it. They won't let him into Britain. Why should they? Are you mad? What do you know? You haven't the faintest idea about anything. You're not even married to the man. Are you getting married?' He stopped suddenly, and then whispered furiously. 'Of course not. I'll tell you what'll happen, shall I? He'll follow your tail to Manila and get stuck there. He won't be able to come back here. You get me? He's got kids, hasn't he? Mad. *Mad.*'

He stood up abruptly. 'I'm going. Come on.'

'Where to?'

'Where's Rafael? At Alphonse's place? Come on.'

'No. I won't! I'm to stay here; he told me.'

'Fine. I'm going anyway. He's a grown man but he's going to listen to me first.'

Emma wiped her eyes angrily as he left the room. 'What business is it of his?'

Valerie shrugged. 'God knows. He gets a bee in his bonnet about things. I expect you could do with a shower?'

Emma's own face, looking in the mirror out of the darkness of the bathroom, gave her a shock. She hadn't looked into any mirror since this same one, the last time in Dumaguete. Lifting it from the hook she carried it to the window, where the evening light seemed to play tricks with colour. Her hair had reddened in the sun, her eyes looked pale in her brown skin, the lashes bleached white. She looked like somebody else.

She showered, washed her shirt and pegged it on the line, then pulled her travel bag from the spare room and emptied its contents over the floor downstairs. All the stuff she had brought from England – lotion, hats, Sartre, her watch.

'Here you go. Any use to you?'

Valerie watched. 'Don't you want to take any of it?'

'Only a couple of things. I want to travel light.'

She shook the bag carefully outside. The night was now fully dark and starry; she could smell the cooking fires. Rafael might appear at any moment and she must be ready.

She packed her toothbrush, shorts, shirts, journal and pens, her shawl over the top. She spread the pale green terno.

'How about this?'

'Don't you want it?'

'Well, it's not really me, is it? I haven't room, anyway.'

'Leave it then. Em, what d'you think Rafael would do, if you got to England? Have you thought?'

'We'll see, won't we? Maybe we won't even go to England. Maybe we'll pick up work somewhere else.'

'You'll need permits and all that.'

'What time is it?'

'Nearly eight. You catching the bus, or what?'

Emma didn't reply. Privately she wondered whether Rafael would come for her at all. She tied the straps of the bag and propped it by the door. That was it then, she was done. Valerie passed her a cigarette.

'Don't suppose you've thought of Alphonse in all of this... Emma?'

'Don't go *on*.'

When Rafael shouldered quietly through the gap in the fence, Alphonse wasn't surprised; he had been waiting. The twilight had found him sitting in the yard, stooped over the crate that served him as a table. He was gently emptying the tobacco from a cigarette by rolling it to and fro between fingers and thumb. He preferred to smoke without tobacco at all but this time he happened to have a cigarette and not much grass, not having ventured far afield in the past few days, not since the message from Mindanao had taken him to Loloy. He had hesitated before going to Loloy, but he had gone. A brother was a brother.

It hadn't been hard to persuade Loloy that two bottles of rum might keep the police force occupied for the duration of a night shift. Finding a driver had taken a little longer. Now he just had to wait.

He divided the tobacco into two and smoothed one half into the open pages of his book. He read, blending the mixture in his palms as he did so. *Our noisy years seem moments in the being/ of the eternal silence.* The Intimations of Wordsworth never failed to give comfort. He rolled up the second half, tucked it into the book, and lit the first. He did not light the lamp.

The English girl had come and gone through his life like a gust of wind. Already she had gone from his mind, even if, technically, she would be passing through Dumaguete one more time, perhaps even now. As far as he was concerned, she was gone. He inhaled. Her time had ripened and fallen from life's tree like a... he searched for a simile... like a guava. Guavas left only a scent. Was it good? Was it bad? It was itself, it was guava. It was nothing. It was something, however, to Rafael. It might take him spinning away, right off the chessboard. Or not.

To play chess, to play Shakespeare. The Shakespeare play. Charles had offered him a part but no, it was beyond him. If it was poetry – he leaned back, blowing a thin stream of smoke straight upwards towards the first stars – if it was poetry then he would leave it up there in the peculiar ether, uncomprehended. However, he would prompt. He would stand at the side and follow the lines over and over and maybe the sense would come. Rafael would soon be crossing, so to speak, centre-stage. This was a metaphor.

Sucking the stub until it glittered, and burning his fingers in the process, Alphonse closed his eyes. He did not sleep. He was listening. When his brother stepped quietly through the gap in the fence, he jumped to his feet at once.

Cita broke the neck of the chicken with a quick twist and thrust the warm bird into the woman's hand. Not for the Romero household, that one, but for the pot of this woman, their laundry-maid, as she had promised. The maid in return had sworn to bring her the news whenever it came, day or night, and here she was, and now she must leave at once; there was a curfew. Cita spat after her. She cursed her for the news and her son also who had watched every boat come in and who said that he had seen them. Ai!

Her moan woke the baby and she gave him her breast. With a trembling hand she reached for the corner of the shelf where the letter lay crumpled, the one from the post office where the white pig had thrown it down. The writing prickled her fingers in the dark; she felt it, she absorbed it. The foreign thing could be pulled into her as her milk could be pulled out; it must be known and met and overcome. She crushed the letter tightly and then, still cradling the child, skewered a nail through the pages. Tomorrow she might burn it, or bury it – but first, before daylight, she must walk to the town and see for herself.

It was halfway through the night. Valerie went to bed at

eleven o'clock, telling Emma to wake her if anything happened. But it was obvious. No journey could begin at such an hour, the curfew began at midnight and there were no buses. Emma didn't lie down; she could barely sit still. She paced about and sat down again, jiggling her knees in agitation, one against the other. *He must come, he has to come, he will come, he must come.* She smoked until the packet was empty, walking the length of the patio up and down, stopping at every turn to peer into the dark.

Then came the sound of a truck on the path, slam, slam, and the next moment they were there, all three of them, Charles, Alphonse, Rafael. Emma? Yes. Good. Ready? Yes. What about the curfew? Is okay. We must. Valerie? Asleep. Wake her. Why are we whispering? This is your bag? Yes. Shall I light the lamp? No.

By the light of a candle cupped in Valerie's hand she saw them all, saw herself as belonging neither with this one nor that – Charles, saying nothing to her now, murmuring only about a last beer but there wasn't time; Valerie, lifting her hair sleepily from her face; Alphonse, stroking his chin with a little smile; Rafael, lifting her bag to his shoulders, for she was going with him now, out of this dim, flickering circle.

Unsa pa? Okay.

The moon was up. She followed him exactly along the path, not past the truck and the neighbouring huts but through the trees. The label on the back of her bag gleamed like an eye. Had she not left something behind? She had broken away so quickly, she had hardly said goodbye.

They were at the edge of the coco palms, some way above the culvert. The road shone dead white under the moon. Rafael set off immediately in the opposite direction, away from the town, keeping to one of the double tracks left by the traffic. His feet made small crunching sounds in the grit. Emma edged towards the side of the road, towards cover, but he shook his head and waved her on. She glanced at his face. How different he looked – who was this man, walking beside her so rapidly and so silent? Why was she so afraid that she could hardly breathe?

They reached the crossroads and paused. Almost at once came the sound of an engine in the distance and Rafael backed into shadow, pulling her after him. A truck approached, showing only one headlight, slowing to a halt some twenty yards away. He touched her arm and they ran to the passenger side of the cab. There was nowhere to put her foot, she must scramble, she was up, she was wedged between Rafael and a man at the wheel she had never seen before and who was slipping up the gears and taking them slowly, grindingly, away.

Fourteen

The crossroads remained empty in the moonlight long after the moon moved on. A snake slid along the dry edge of the road; there were bats overhead and cockerels screeching here and there before the dawn.

A woman appeared at last along a path and paused at the dividing of the road. It was Cita, her small figure bent forward slightly under the weight of the baby on her back. She seemed to sniff the air, which was cool and sweet. Then she continued towards the town.

When Emma awoke they were still driving north along the coast and it was still night. The single headlight tracked on through the sleeping barrios, past fields of cane and under acres of palm. A faint streak showed in the sky as she glimpsed the sea; she must have slept for an hour or so. Her thigh was pressed against Rafael's, hip to knee. She would be needing a toilet soon. Otherwise she could travel on through the dark between these two men, always.

No one spoke; the motor was too noisy. A picture of the Virgin Mary flapped from the driver's mirror, her pious gaze, drunk with holiness, showing more and more clearly in the growing light.

All at once Emma knew where they were. The shape of the mountain on the left was familiar; it was Canlaon, the volcano. Perhaps extinct, perhaps not. They would be in San Carlos soon. She thought of Dolores, wondered if Colorado had seemed so amazing on her return; wondered, too, about Ellis. Had he ever turned up? Valerie and Charles had not mentioned him. The outskirts of San Carlos appeared at the next corner. Some memory about the place connected with the report she had read about sorcery – what was the word that Ellis had used? She felt Rafael tense beside her. It was barely light. What time did the curfew end?

Rafael leaned forward and spoke into her ear.

'Sorry?'

'Money. He leave us here. We pay him, okay?'

She found her purse and handed it to him, pressing herself back into the seat as the two men spoke, as Rafael handed money across and the driver swerved past a dog, past a group of women with flat baskets of fruit on their heads, grey in the half-light. When they stopped it was in the same market as before, where Emma had parted from Dolores. The same buses hunkered down in the dust, the same little stores were opening like caves onto the plaza. They jumped down, waved goodbye.

'Unsang orasa na?'

She took her watch from her pocket and showed him.

'Bakut ko. Sige. Paeskina kita. Let's go to the corner. Usa pa.' He read the notices jammed into the bus windows. 'This one. Bacolod.' He opened his hands. 'Soon-soon.'

In the toilet there was nowhere dry to put her bag, no paper, no flush, only the usual water barrel half full, and a paint tin for a scoop. As she stepped outside again and failed to see him, fear came back – a sudden hammering in her chest. But there he was, buying something from a stall. They climbed up into the bus and sat in silence. I love it, she thought, that he speaks so seldom, but it keeps surprising me all the same. I'm not used to it.

When the engine roared into life and the bus pulled through the town he slapped his hands down on his knees and let out a long breath.

'Okay,' he said. 'Is okay now.'

'Maglagot ako niha!'

The old woman pursed her lips and rocked slowly from side to side. Ah-ah-ah-ah. Yes, you hate her! So? They are gone. Cita stood before her, her dress ripped from the neck to the waist. Mamatay ako! she cried. I will die.

The skinny hands took hold of her shoulders and gripped her firmly, then gathered up the dress. Eh, put your tits away and listen to me. What do you wish on her? The most terrible thing you could wish. Dead? Puh! A long life can be worse. Come, come, the fire is going out.

Cita knocked the glowing husks apart and pushed another husk between them. Her grandmother broke leaves into the pot and stirred for a while before she spoke again. Maybe he is not leaving because of the foreign woman. Maybe he is not leaving because of you. He is just leaving. He is a man.

She tipped the liquid from the pot into a cup. Take it, drink it. Listen. You have children. The other one is – she rubbed her belly – empty. That is the pebble lying at the bottom of the river; keep it in your mind's eye. Whatever you wish on her – she has done it already to herself, ten times over.

Emma stared out of the bus as they arrived in Bacolod. Another town. Another place of shops, markets, and a harbour; full of other lives she would never see or know, passing through and moving on as she would. It was late afternoon. She was cramped, sticky and dusty after the ride, as if she had crossed a desert. It felt wonderful. What happened next – where they would sleep that night, for example – she did not ask. It would reveal itself in good time. She was with Rafael; it was enough.

He set off through the streets, asking directions now and again. They came to an old but well-to-do neighbourhood and stopped outside a large house. There was a lawn, a wrought-iron balcony and a peeling facade. My cousin's, he said. You've been here before? she asked. He shook his head. He took off his hat, folding it into his pocket and smoothing down his hair. So.

The maid who answered their knock stared at them open-mouthed and then remembered herself, going to fetch the mistress of the house. She returned with an austere, Spanish-looking woman, rather tall for a Filipina, who frowned at Rafael's introductions. After a moment's silence, she ushered them inside.

They were separated at once, Emma to the maid's quarters with the maid. The girl patted one of three narrow beds and gave Emma a sideways smile, pointing to a wash-house outside in the yard. Emma nodded and pointed to herself. My name: Emma. The girl flashed another smile and left the room, her slippers flapping on the tiled floor.

Washed and as tidy as possible, given the crumpled state of her best skirt, Emma stood cautiously in the passage. It was, for a Filipino household, unusually quiet. She walked towards the hall. Somewhere to her left she heard voices, one of which she guessed belonged to the lady of the house. It seemed best not to interrupt. A lizard skittered on the wall, making her jump. She retreated, and sat down in the maid's room.

A whistle sounded from outside.

'Pustorawo, no?' Rafael raised his eyebrows when he saw her wearing a skirt. 'We go out, after, sige ha? But first, we eat here. It is necessary.'

In a long, spare dining room, where Jesus raised bleeding hands on the walls and flies spun in the air, they lowered their eyes while grace was said. The aunt presided, briefly introducing Emma to the two men and an elderly woman who joined them at the table, and then asking questions in stiffly correct English. Why had she come to the Philippines, for it was such a poor country? And why did she come without her family?

As meat was served, Rafael interceded on her behalf. None for her; it was against her religion. Emma gave him a quick, grateful look, which sent a wave of desire and love pouring through her. The aunt's carving knife remained poised in the air for a moment; behind her, the eyes of Jesus swam with sorrow.

I mustn't assume anything, Emma reminded herself, picking her way through the meal. He is nice to me, we get along. I have offered him a chance to leave the country, that's all. No reason to think that he wants *me*.

When the maid had removed the last of the dishes and the other diners had moved away, Emma stood behind her chair uncertainly. Rafael was speaking but she could not follow what he said. Then he turned to her with the familiar beckoning scoop of his hand. 'Mamasiyo kita.'

Once outside the gate, they began to walk. It was early evening, and dark. Down to the harbour, finding it bigger than Dumaguete, past the cranes and sheds and huge hulls of ships. Rafael hailed an official who stood on the wharf, and nodded when he received a reply. They turned back towards the town, following sidestreets and alleys, going nowhere, just walking.

'We have a drink, yes?'

'Yes. Tuba?'

'They may not have. Is not, you say, common? Sibukay, yes. Plenty coconut, plenty tuba. Bacolod, no. Pero, we try.'

He asked in several of the shacks which stood, each lit by a paraffin lamp, open to the street. Eventually he waved her inside. They sat at a tiny table in the half-dark, with glasses of the thick, strong stuff between them. It tasted different, it had been brought by boat from somewhere, but it was delicious. He fetched second glasses, chinking his own against hers, sliding the change across the table.

Finding their way back to the house later, and looking at its windows and its closed door, they decided to stay outside for a while. The lawn was a white sheet in the moonlight. It was only natural to lie down on it. God, that moon. A moon so huge and globular and full of meaning, powering down into them. They lay flat out, a couple of feet apart, maybe not so much. Twenty inches. Twenty inches of grass and moon, Emma noted wonderingly – *I can reach across them without moving a muscle, and the world is full of mystery and I am full of happiness.* They shared a cigarette, remaining there until the lights in the lower windows of the house went out. He stood up, stretching like a cat. Tomorrow night, he said, the boat leave. For Manila. Sa buntag, we buy tickets.

MANILA. My journal has been at the bottom of my bag; I've written nothing since leaving Sibukay. Leaving Dumaguete, the harbour at Bacolod in the morning with you to secure tickets and

*that feeling: nothing could go wrong, and every moment it grew
more and more. I thought of a day when it rained in London and
I sat in a café on the corner of Carnaby Street, scribbling the
badness out of me, seeing that the very shape of a human being was
an ugly thing, and the lights too bright, the sounds too loud. In the
ticket office at Bacolod, the opposite. Everything shone. The smell
of a harbour. The songs on someone's radio were familiar and each
one better than the last, the temperature was perfect, the state of
indecision easy on the mind, the babble of humanity infinitely
intriguing, the book I read made me laugh out loud; the human
form seemed a magnificent thing. The man at his desk thumbing
through timetables – he amazed me with his concentration, it must
have been interesting; the phones jangled, the clerks lazed idly in
their chairs, every face had character and so much beauty and the
whole scene came together like a master plan.*

*On the boat – the dark, windy deck and rain, and very hungry,
watching the sun rising between islands – I'll have that one, you
have that one. Now Manila, and another cousin's house, another
uncle and aunt, another bed in the maid's room, and my doubts
still remain but happiness too. Sorry that I sit too close to you! I
can't help myself, the affection just comes out of me and I've done
it before I can think better of it. Coming to sit beside you this
morning – you newly wakened and wrapped in a blanket, exuding
night and sleep, and all of me longs to turn and open my arms.*

Emma stopped writing as the door opened and Beatriz,
the maid, came in. She sat down on the opposite bed,
looking at Emma with a frank stare. After a moment she

pulled one bra strap from beneath the sleeve of her shirt, followed by the other. Undoing the hooks at the back, she lifted the bra out at the neckline, folded it away and then lay down with her back to Emma and her face to the wall.

It was evening, their second evening in the city. Dark, but not yet late, some amorphous time between supper and sleep. The men were downstairs, Rafael and his uncle, Ramon Quirino, and a young man whose name sounded like Ano, or Arno, who might be his son-in-law. The aunt was out at a church meeting, the daughter cloistered in her room. Downstairs, Emma guessed, the men would be smoking, reading newspapers, making small talk, the fan turning with a thwack and shudder on the ceiling, and mosquitoes seeking out the holes in the netting at the window. She had joined them the night before and their talk had changed uneasily into English, Rafael sitting on the edge of his chair, stiff in this new urban setting.

A snore came from Beatriz, although the light from the bare bulb still blazed down. Outside, an occasional car passed the gate, through which a blue glow could be seen from a neon sign further down the road. Beyond that, street after street of the district, Cubao. It was a city but it wasn't like London, it was nothing like London; the hot, strong smells could only be on the other side of world.

Uncle Ramon coughed in the room below. He had not been very encouraging, so far, about their plans to leave the country. He had crossed and re-crossed his legs in silence, snatching at a fly, and finally shrugged. He had nothing to suggest. It was difficult. These were difficult times.

A cockroach ran into the shadows under the bed. Emma took a magazine from a pile on the dresser and turned the pages. Pretty girls, a quiz, prayers. Recipes in English and in Tagalog. An article, 'The Blessing of Marriage'. She began to read.

A little later she lay back and stared ahead. She had read all the articles in the church magazines which were in English and their message was clear and firm. Modern girls sometimes gave in to the temptations of their boyfriends, but sex was always regretted by a woman if she 'fell' before marriage. Happiness was found only through wifely devotion; there was no other route.

A door opened downstairs and, a moment later, the outer gate creaked on its hinges, clattering shut. Another door opened and closed in the house. Beatriz breathed regularly in, out. Emma sat up and listened. No voices from below, just the rattling fan. She went down and found Ramon alone, reading. He nodded to her as she went by. Outside in the corner of the yard a cigarette glowed in the dark and Rafael whistled. She sat beside him on the ground, accepting the cigarette and inhaling meditatively. If the women in the Philippines thought along the lines of the magazines, so did the men – so did this man.

Footsteps sounded in the street; cars passed between one main road and another. Rafael slapped at a mosquito.

'Ramon say he ask tomorrow, about passport. At his

office. But he say – kuan? Magkawangon.' The cigarette, in his hand again, moved from side to side. 'No good.'

The uncle's predictions might be pessimistic, but they needn't be put off by that; they had hardly begun. She said nothing. Presently he rubbed the stub out between his fingers and murmured, 'I have another uncle. Ugma sa buntag, we try him.'

Fifteen

Rafael woke up. The girl Beatriz had awakened him as she came downstairs and prepared to go to market. Her every movement in the kitchen let him know that she knew he was awake, that he was a man lying there on the sofa on the other side of the room and that he was in the way. Presently she passed close by the sofa and he heard the sound of the bolts drawn on the front door. He kept his eyes closed until he heard the gate swing shut.

The sun sliced through the window screens in thin, sharp lines. The city had changed his sleeping and waking habits already; he hadn't seen the sunrise for a week. In Dumaguete and in Sibukay he had not missed the sunrise and he had not been plagued by dreams. Now he dreamed of his brother standing on the deck of a ship, calling. He dreamed of his woman plaiting their daughter's hair, and she would not look at him, and the girl's face, too, was turned away.

He swore under his breath, and shut his eyes again. The

pterygium in the right eye bothered him, the light in
Manila was unforgiving, bouncing as it did from walls and
flat surfaces, making him long for trees. Maybe it was the
dust, irritating his eyes. Closing them, he saw Cita again
and her quick, slim fingers in the black hair. Meanwhile
the English girl slept in the room above, or perhaps also lay
awake and thought of him. He knew, now, that she thought
of him. Of course. Why else would he be here? But he had
not been sure, and now he was sure.

The day before, at the offices of his uncle in Makati,
he had seen incredulity on the other man's face. Passport?
he had cried, staring at Rafael – for *you*? He spoke
about money, thousands and thousands of pesos; it was
quite impossible. He had not said that his nephew was a
loafer from the provinces, from the backwoods; it was so
obviously true.

He had stood with Emma in the descending lift, and the
two of them had walked out through the reception area
like a pair of vagabonds. Yet she could never be a vagabond;
she was English. On impulse they had entered a movie
house and sat side by side in the dark. *The Godfather* with
sub-titles had deepened the enigma of which he found
himself so mysteriously a part. Re-emerging into the
blazing glare of Ayala Avenue and crossing the street in the
rush hour traffic, he had grabbed her hand, as he would
have held onto anyone. On the opposite pavement he had
not dropped his hand away, neither had she. It was done.
Later in the evening, as they sat on a wall at the street

corner, he had found her mouth with his, to be absolutely certain.

He rose to his feet now, folding the sheet with neat, economic movements and sliding it out of the way. It was necessary to use the bathroom before the rest of the household; that he and Emma were a burden to them, he was well aware. His cousin Isabela was engaged to be married; the forthcoming wedding meant that savings had to be made all round. Naturally he was welcome as a family member, naturally a foreigner was a guest; good manners would be upheld. But it was an uncomfortable situation for them all.

The table had been laid for breakfast already. He would like, now, to make a fire and set a pot of rice over it, but the cooking stove in the corner was something quite different, and it wasn't his business to touch it. Besides, it was perhaps provincial to eat rice for breakfast. He caught sight of his face in the mirror at the foot of the stairs, and pushed down an unruly bit of hair. He missed wearing his hat. He examined his face more closely, trying to imagine it on a plane, leaving the country. Just then a noise from above sent him diving for the sofa, where he sat tense and alert, staring at a magazine.

His uncle descended, bent double by a fit of coughing and shutting himself into the bathroom. Emma's face appeared over the banisters, rosy and smiling. She looked at Rafael transfixed for a second while the sounds of gargling and hawking issued from behind the door; then she crossed the room and sat beside him, her knee against his. He kissed her quickly. The outer gate clanged and Beatriz entered, her arms full of packages and her eyes missing nothing.

''buntag.'

'Good morning.'

'Good morning.'

Ramon took his seat with a sigh, turning on the radio and feeling in his pockets. Rafael declined the proffered cigarette, although he very much wanted one. *You are listening to VWRV, Radio Veritas.* They listened respectfully to the news, waiting for Isabela. Ramon's wife did not take breakfast.

Ramon Quirino presided at the table with heavy-lidded eyes. He blessed the food in Tagalog and then led the conversation in English for the sake of his guest, the young English woman who had hair as flat and colourless as the Pasig River. She had come to his house for no reason he could easily fathom, having apparently spent months in the Philippines, yet knowing nothing. Neither the name of Fidel Ramos, nor even Ninoy Aquino.

He shook his head and toyed with the papaya on his plate. She spoke well enough, she was *edukado*, it was good for Isabela to practise her English. But as for his nephew's rather hesitant claim that she was a writer – well, anyone of sensitivity could look into her eyes and know that this was not so. His nephew, meanwhile (Ramon sighed again);

he was a piece hewn straight from the islands of the south, if ever there was one.

Isabela asked many questions. She wanted to know the population of London and the minimum average temperature of the English winters in Fahrenheit. She seemed really to be interested. The names and ages of the Queen's children she already knew. Emma was nonplussed. This was a new mix of east and west, an anomaly. What did anomaly mean? Was there a dictionary in the house? How could she concentrate with her own darling sitting at the end of the table, with his thin moustache and his lips which had kissed her?

The fork should not be laid back on the tablecloth, but on the plate. Neither straight up, nor across, but at an angle. With the knife. But he had not used a knife. Rafael paused, looking around and catching Emma's eye. She seemed to fill with a pink dye, so rapidly did the colour flush over her face.

Ramon caught the look which passed between them, and fiddled with his napkin.

They caught a bus at the main road, squeezing together into a seat at the back. Traffic swelled around them, horns blared, music blared; the sun blared over their heads. They were looking for the Overseas Workers Welfare Administration, why not? Hundreds of Filipinos had contracts to work abroad; maybe thousands left the country that way. A trickle of sweat ran down between Emma's breasts and into the waistband of her shorts. She was used to it. She fanned her face with a piece of cardboard and tapped her feet to the music. She didn't care about a thing. At the same time she cared for everything very much, it was very dear to her, the bright and lovely world surging past – no, not surging past now but gathering her up and taking her along.

'How do I say: I feel happy?'

'Mubati akog kalipay. Or, gaan ang buot.'

'Gaan ang buot?'

'O-o. In a happy mood.'

She whispered it to herself, covering her mouth against the dust. She whispered it to the street cleaners in their conical hats, to the Virgin Mary flapping above the driver, to the words of the song which came loudly from his stereo. *On a dark desert highway, cool wind in my hair. Gaan ang buot, gaan ang buot.*

It was a long walk. Rafael knew the area a little from the time he had worked on the American air base, when he and Alphonse had spent a few weeks showing some service-men a very different side of Manila. He had learned much of his English then and also something of the ways of foreigners.

That was years ago and it all looked different now. This crossroads, for instance, might be too far to the west.

They could catch another bus, but his sense of economy argued against this. It wasn't his own money they spent on fares every day but it was the only money they had in the world and it might be needed for greater distances. Emma had said that it was a limited supply; they must not squander it by riding around the city.

On the other hand it was hot and she was tired. He felt it, as she walked at his side. Making a sudden decision he led her towards a tiny store that looked and felt like an oven, speaking to the youth inside, who fetched glasses.

'Water? Or Pepsi?'

'Are we nearly there?'

'Not far.'

'Better have water, do you think? Tubig, salamaat.'

She looked longingly at a faded picture of a Pepsi Cola bottle lying on a bed of ice. The water was warm and milky and a persistent fly settled over and over again on the rim of her glass. Phoo. Okay now. She was ready.

The skyline was different in this part of town. No towering offices or banks but small buildings with their doorways full of garbage. A heap of dwellings leaned together on a piece of wasteground like kennels, each with a cooking fire outside and people, people, people. Still in bright colours, still playing guitars.

'Diretso.' He pointed. Overseas Workers, said the sign. The office was small and busy and hot, its floors littered and its walls hung with lists in Tagalog and English. It reminded her of a betting shop. She searched the lists.

There – London: *Nanny. Nurse. Cleaner.* Her eyes moved on. Japan: *Hostess. Dancer. Hostess.* There seemed to be nothing for men. Ah, Oman. *Construction Worker. Age 18-30.* No good, he was older than that. And what use would it be, for him to become a construction worker under contract in Oman?

She sat on a bench, where a fan on the counter stirred the air slightly. His back was towards her as he scanned the list, and she knew from the way he stood that this was hopeless. He spoke to another man, shrugged, shook his head and turned back to her with a wave of his hands. Come.

Dear mummy. We are on Roxas Boulevard which is by Manila Bay. There's a big new building called the Cultural Centre in front of us and palm trees and people walking up and down. Late afternoon so it's still very hot but bearable. We've been finding out about the chances of Rafael getting a job abroad and the place we've been to wasn't the main office apparently but he was told that the jobs are the same even in the main office and not suitable. The men's jobs are fixed contract so they pay your fare out of the Philippines and then back again so that's no good. We'll try the British Embassy next and I'm sure they will help us.

We're waiting for it to get cooler before we get a bus back to Cubao where his uncle lives and I can post this on the way. Anyway I'm fine and the mosquito bites are much better and they don't seem to bother me any more now. Love, Emmie.

She folded the letter, writing her mother's address on the envelope and realising that she was sending her selected information only. Nothing about the confusion which gripped her from time to time. Like the night before.

Isabela's fiancé had arrived at the house with two friends and had sat with Ramon and Rafael, drinking beer. Isabela and her mother, a slim, elegant Filipina with an immaculate coiffure, had vanished. Beatriz, off duty, had flip-flopped down the street. Emma belonged neither here nor there, nowhere. It was unseemly to sit alone at the corner of the street, and perhaps unsafe. The men had talked, opening more bottles. She said goodnight, seeing a fleeting concern in Rafael's eyes, by then more blood-shot than ever. Then he smiled and tipped the bottle. She might have imagined a look of concern that wasn't there at all. When he was drunk he was in another world, and she was shut out. She thought of Alphonse with a pang. Upstairs, the maid's room had hummed under the bulb, and the cockroaches rasped their nasty nail-like wings in the corners.

She put the letter away now and leaned her head back against the wall. This morning his eyes had been bleary but he was sober, he was with her again and they had a shared purpose. Now he was having a late siesta, his face covered by the spotted handkerchief. She must not worry. It was English to worry. The traffic roared behind them, the bay turned from gold to pink as the sun dropped.

'Magsawop na ang adlaw.'

She gave a little start. He had spoken through his scarf, which he now lifted.

'Magsa — what?'

'Magsawop na ang adlaw. Magabii na.'

She shook her head. 'Adlaw? Meaning 'day'?'

'O-o. The sun will be setting soon.'

He stood up. He had not been asleep. Siesta was not always just for sleep but for returning into oneself. Behind the handkerchief he knew that she was there, busily writing, busy in her mind. His own thoughts neither moved around her nor ferreted into the future at such times, nor pondered any of it at all.

It was rush hour again. The pavements seethed, the jeepneys crawled through the traffic, the buses flashed coloured lights and music. He took hold of her hand firmly. *I was thinking to myself, this could be heaven or this could be hell.* He understood it perfectly, these words they heard on every bus and every pavement, this song from the other side. Alphonse would listen to such words with his head on one side and smile at them, filing them away for quotation. *We are all just prisoners here of our own device.* Bitaw; indeed. Her hand lay trustingly in his like a small, sweating animal.

The consular secretary's clerk, whose name was Anderson, blew his nose. Air conditioning created a mucus problem. Other than that, his acclimatising to the Third World had taken place pretty smoothly, all things considered, thanks to the tips from Spurling at the top.

He looked out over the hazy sprawl of Manila and then adjusted the shades at the window. The light was very harsh; it could damage the retina. That individual who had sat in a T-shirt on that very chair just now was a case in point. His eyes had been in a frightful mess. Exacerbated by drink, no doubt. Odd business, that couple. But the official guidelines were quite clear.

Emma had never felt so humiliated. Had never felt so deeply, dreadfully humiliated down into her soul. What a horrid man. The further they walked and the more she thought about it, the more shameful it became. Who did he think he was, a jumped-up Foreign Office squirt like that, with a shirt and tie and a pointy face, sitting behind a desk? He had hardly given them the time of day. He had addressed every question to her, as if Rafael couldn't speak for himself. And he had said, in the most damning and patronising way; *we wouldn't let him into Britain.* And if we get married? she had asked, her heart in her mouth. The man had actually given a little laugh. *We still wouldn't let him in. And by the way,* he had added, sliding her passport back across the desk towards her, *you have overstayed your visa. You'd better see to it.*

Thank you, she replied stiffly. Seconds later they were back on the street. There was nothing to say. They would walk back to Cubao. Hang the heat.

So, mused Rafael. She is very fierce. She is surprised by her own countryman. He asks, what is her profession? She says, writer. He replies, oh yes. He asks me, what is my profession? And I have no answer. She should not be surprised.

He looked ahead. The traffic was not flowing as usual and a crowd had gathered at the bridge over the Pasig. She had seen nothing, just shifted her bag from one shoulder to the other. They walked on. As they drew nearer to the crowd, he put out a hand to stop her.

'Wait.'

'What?'

'Usa pa. You wait.'

He went on ahead. She watched his figure walking away and then looked around for some shade. There was none. Her feet were sticky in the sandals and she slipped them off, standing barefoot. She could no longer see him. She thought of that petty official again, dishing out the mores of superiority. *We wouldn't let him into Britain.* That, compared with the kindness she had been given lately – Nanay, pushing food onto her plate, saying kaon pa! kaon pa! Have some more! And concentrating over her sewing machine, making clothes for the foreigner...

There he was. He shook his head as he joined her. 'We go another way.'

'What is it?'

'There are some killed.'

'Killed? What d'you mean?'

'There.' He waved his hand upriver. 'Two body. In the river.'

'Why can't we go that way?'

'Is not for you.'

'I'm not afraid.'

'Is not for you. We go this way. Magsakay kita.'

He hurried her into a passing jeepney which had slowed for the traffic at the corner. She crouched and pressed past the knees of other passengers inside while he remained on the footplate, hanging on with one hand. A sudden jolt flung her over someone's lap. Sorry, sorry! Excuse me. There were smiles in the half-light as she peered from her corner. Was he still there? Of course. She drew a deep breath and as she exhaled, shed a few tears. She blinked them back. He would think that she was upset about death lying there in the river in the middle of the city, but it wasn't that. It was that man, that awful Englishman who had shamed her.

On the steps of the post office in Cubao they could sit for hours undisturbed, watching the night fall. Her hand on his thigh was no longer just comradely, although it was that, too. It was becoming a problem. They had, simply, nowhere private to go. Sooner or later they must return to the Quirino house where the family had to chaperone their guest; odd though she was, she was *dalaga*, unmarried.

Rafael covered her hand with his, pressing it into his groin. 'Perhaps we go to Alacay. I know people there, I have address. Perhaps they have a place for us, no?'

'Another uncle?'

He smiled. 'Cousin, tingali.'

'You have big families.'

'Bitaw. And when a friend is good, he become cousin.'

'In England we say: he is like a brother to me.'

'In Philippine, no. A brother is a brother.'

She drew her hand away. 'Where do these people live?'

'Alacay.'

'Is it far?'

'Quite far.'

Sixteen

The best times are the mornings, waking early, knowing you are downstairs and I can creep down and kiss you before Beatriz sees. Nightfall in Manila, dawn in Manila. Dust, noise, the faces, you — you reading the paper, you coming out of the shower, you wearing my dark glasses, you smoothing my hair away, more gentle than any. All my distrust gone, knowing you better. In the evenings we sit by the road in silence and you leave me to my thoughts and I keep myself whole and not drained away, only secured by knowing you are still there. I don't want to leave you. I haven't said that for so long, it sounds strange.

It was another long bus ride to Alacay, this time away from the city. The highway was under construction but the traffic already boiled up the dust in the web of bare metal and grit. When they climbed down it was in the middle of neither streets nor wasteland, but an uncertain compromise between the two. Rafael made enquiries, then, wrapping his scarf around his eye to shield it from the glare, he once more took her hand.

He asked again for directions. There – some wooden houses around a few banana trees and a communal tap – that one, in the corner. He whistled at the low door. A youngish man with a fresh, newly awakened face parted the fly-curtain, a towel around his middle. La! he cried, seeing Emma and disappearing at once back into the house. They waited. Presently he re-emerged in shorts and a T-shirt and with a huge, happy smile, pressing Rafael's hands.

'Siloy! This, Emma. Emma, is Siloy. He say his wife, Adoracion, she at work. Sige! Come.'

The room had a table, three chairs, a cooking stove and a concrete floor. There was no window, only a deep, cool shade. Siloy gave rapid orders to a small child at the door who nodded, running off across the yard on bare feet and returning minutes later with a cool bottle of San Miguel gripped in each fist. Siloy opened these with his teeth. When Rafael offered his to Emma, Siloy jumped to his feet. No, no, Rafael waved him back into his seat. It was okay, Emma had shaken her head. The beer would make her sleepy. Water would do fine. What she really fancied was a bowl of Coco Pops with fresh, ice-cold milk.

The boy was sent for more beer. She pointed to her purse and raised her eyebrows. Rafael nodded. The men talked. *I have sat at so many tables like this*, she thought. *Heard so many conversations I've not understood – not that it matters;*

it is very restful not to understand — with so many bus rides in the dust, so many faces smiling at me, so much sun pouring down outside. It can't go on forever. She shuddered. His hand came towards her, not quite touching. I'm all right, she reassured him. It was the first time she had thought it: *It can't go on forever.*

A second room lay behind the first, Siloy and Adoracion's bedroom, with a cubicle to one side made of plywood and with a single bunk. This was, Rafael explained to her later, a sleeping space added for a nephew. This nephew would be away for two nights because it was the weekend and so they, Rafael and Emma, could stay here, together, now, tonight; was this okay? Yes, she nodded. Yes.

All afternoon, they wondered how it would be. Shopping in the straggling market with its stalls almost empty at the end of the day, with paraffin lamps flaring here and there in the twilight, they wondered. Sibuyas, onions. Itlog, egg. She put money into his hands, and thought about how his hands would feel. He considered some cabbage, and decided against it. He carried fish, wrapped in newspaper, packing the vegetables into her bag, and he also wondered.

At the house, he helped to cook. Siloy dandled a baby on his lap while Emma sat at the table, feeling useless, watching Rafael with a mixture of love and dread. After the meal she tried to do the washing up, but the water was cold in the bucket and she wasn't sure about using soap, or about how much rinsing was expected, or where to put the plates to drain. Adoracion, shy and round with pregnancy, shooed her away.

'What does she say?'

'She say, maybe her baby have nose like you, because you stay here.'

'A nose like mine?'

'O-o. Ilong. Like this.' He sketched a nose in the air.

'She believes that?'

'No, no. She teach English, here, in the school.'

'Does she? She doesn't speak English to me.'

'She is modest. She is Filipina. You have cigarette?'

Emma shook her head. He sent the boy with a few cen-tavos for a cigarette, lighting it at the candle on the table. She followed every movement, the curve of his hand around the flame, the arch of his back, the gesture of his head towards the door: come. They sat in the dark, passing the cigarette from his fingers to hers and back again.

It was hot in the cubicle. Emma used the washhouse out-side first; Rafael had to lock the door behind them both. She stood in the dark, listening to the murmurings of their hosts. She felt her way forward slowly and bumped her shins on the bunk. The walls shook. Her hands found a folded sheet of some kind. To take all her clothes off, or not? She took off her shorts and shirt and lay down in her underwear, pulling the sheet up to her chin.

She heard the door close and the bolts pushed across. He appeared in the doorway with the candle; strange angles

lit across his face before he blew it out. She heard the
sounds of his clothing as he folded it, the sound of his feet
wiped on the mat, felt his cautious touch feeling for where
she was, her stomach, her breasts, her face, and then lifting
the sheet. She put out her arm and knocked his shoulder.
Okay, okay, he whispered. His fingers found her lips. Okay.
She ran her hands in amazement down his back at last. It
was breathlessly hot. She took off her bra. He kissed her
lightly, tentatively; wrapped his arms around her.

'We go to the beach, no? You want?'

They sat down to breakfast. Siloy and his wife had eaten
already and an egg, fried for Emma, lay cold on a plate in
the middle of the table, covered by another plate to keep
off the flies. In another saucer, also covered, some fish. Rice
in a pot, water in a jug. The four legs of the table stood in
dishes of water; a long band of ants tracked the wall. Yes, she
would like to go to the beach more than anything.

It was a short ride to Cavite and, being a Saturday, there
was a holiday mood in the air. Far across Manila Bay giant
tankers glimmered in the heat and thick yellow clouds sat
over the suburbs. Small waves broke on the sand. She began
to make a castle, like a child.

'Do we have to go back to Manila?' she asked him.

'O-o.'

'When?'

'Sa hapon. Pero, we can come back to Alacay, no? Siloy
take the family to Cebu for Christmas. We stay at their

place. I ask already. They say, is okay for us.'

He was relieved about this. It might have been awkward in Cubao over Christmas. Siloy's place was okay for them; it was fine. Pagkahuman – afterwards, it was a big problem. He couldn't get out of the country, that was clear. Meanwhile, every day, they spent more of her money.

'We swim again, no?'

He swam a long way, letting the tension out of his body. When he went back to her she was already sitting on the sand again.

'I would like to get married,' she said suddenly. He dried his hair before replying.

'That is what I want, also.'

Beatriz sat up. *That* one thought that she was still asleep but she was awake, Sunday or not. It might be her morning off but she was of course awake and had heard the white woman creep to the door and down the stairs to join Rafael Romero on the sofa.

She crossed herself. She didn't know what the sisters at the convent would say about it, but they would speak of the forgiveness of sin. Oh, it was sinful. It was fornication, surely the whole family must know, and with the daughter of the house engaged to be married, too. Beatriz knew something of the sweet agony Isabela endured to remain chaste.

Now this, this rumpus on the sofa under their roof. The house no longer attended early mass due to various indispositions, which was a pity. Beatriz could not go down to prepare breakfast, as they fasted before the Eucharist on a Sunday. Neither was there any market; she could not shop.

She looked across at the empty bed. There wasn't a sound from below. She could go downstairs to the bathroom. In fact, that was just what she needed to do.

Behind the wall, in a small bedroom with the door slightly ajar to allow for the movement of air, Ramon Quirino heard more than Beatriz thought, and cared rather less than she supposed. His mind was taken up with the lists his wife presented to him – or rather, announced that she had made or would shortly make and which were all quite indispensable. Invitation cards. Serviettes. Nosegays. The banns. The service. The catering. Before all this, Christmas. Her family visiting, as usual. He guessed that his nephew would vacate the sofa before then. Grown man – good luck to him.

He felt a cough rising up from the bottom of his soul and raised himself on one elbow for the onslaught. His wife, turned away, slept on. She was used to his chest. Isabela too, in her room, slept deeply as a healthy girl should. He sat up slowly, braced himself for the next cough then poured a measure of expectorant from a medicine bottle on the bedside table. Footsteps padded past the door. Beatriz, been trying to catch them at it.

*Dear mummy. We went to the Immigration HQ today to pay for
an extension of my visa. Someone took my papers and then we
realised that she was an agent working for a private commission,
so we took everything back. Everyone else seemed to be out for
lunch. Finally I found the commissioner's office upstairs – he was
out for lunch for three hours! When he came back he asked for my
passport, I said that he already had it, he said no I had it, no I
haven't yes you have it's in that drawer... oh yes, so it is. I paid
for his signature, then paid head tax, and something mysterious
called ACR... and then ERC... then 20 pesos per extra month
and 80 pesos for overstaying the original visa, then payment was
stamped in one office and the stamp stamped in another office – !*

She read it back to herself. It sounded quite amusing,
anecdotal, as if it were all a kind of game. That's what
comedians did; they made the truth sound funny. They
omitted things. She had not said, for instance, that her six
months were up, that she had been told to arrange her
onward ticket, that the thought of leaving was killing her.

She saw that in the middle of the paragraph she had
changed *we* to *I*. She lifted her head for a moment, and
then pushed the letter into her journal. Turning to the last
entry she continued to write, this time to herself.

Rafael folded the newspaper. Inactivity was difficult. Here
in the city, it was difficult. He had looked at some books
on English grammar, a gift from Isabela, but it was hard to
concentrate.

In that place today, that immigration place, he'd felt the alienation of it all very sharply. The offices, with their stairs, notices, desks, smart people, and above all, money – it was not his world. Nor did he want it to be. Nor could it be, even if he did so want.

He stood up and went into the kitchen. She sat writing at the table, his woman now. She stopped writing when she saw him and covered the words as if by chance with one hand. He raised his eyebrows. Wala; she shook her head. Nothing. Nothing is the matter. He stooped to kiss her on the forehead.

Soon they would move to Alacay and in Siloy's place they could live ipon-ipon, as husband and wife, for the two weeks of Christmas. After that, there was nowhere left to go, no more time. Walay mahino. But maybe they would think of something.

In his heart he knew that they would not, that the tide was drawing away. He wanted to drink. He would go out tonight and drink. He couldn't take her with him. He couldn't keep her with him at all.

December 13th. What can I think when you come back drunk – it's not for me to approve or not, though right now better not to waste money, but then it's the human reaction, isn't it? To the trap, even of our own making. Something in me says: be careful! I am unsteady.

If I read these words twenty years from now and I am not with you, then am I thankful? Or do I wish it were otherwise? How can I answer it now? I want no child, but I'd like a child of mine to be of you too. In England I'm finished now — I might live for years and find a comfortable place, a job, friends, but I don't want to be without you and whatever I have with you that gives me whatever it is — we are no good for each other but I want part of you, I'd love it, Lord I'd love it so — I wonder if you'd hate me if you knew the thoughts in my head?

December 14th. The thought of having your child makes me ache. I can't explain. I'm bad at decisions — how can I decide this? You say let's just go to Palawan and disappear together. And you have children already, I keep forgetting. You come close to me and wipe it all away — but I'm stronger than you, stronger and more awful. I'm dangerously awful. There's this thing in me knocking about with clenched fists. I need to look you straight in the eye and see the same thing reflected there exactly...

December 16th. Don't give me any of this 'You'll destroy your life too'! Come on, I trust you now, I approach you freely with confidence — maybe you'll prove that to be stupid. I don't think so.

December 17th. The President's speech in Rizal Park. Imelda has sad eyes. But Marcos, I think he believes in his own words. You are reminded of Hitler; I'm thinking of Jesus. You won't talk about it, you bite my shoulder. It doesn't concern us, so it's not worth talking about, is that it? But I'm going to need someone to talk to, and I mean TALK, long and hard. Fair enough. Filipino ikaw. I mustn't forget. Stay that way.

December 19th. Alacay. You gently wake me. I have you near me peaceful and timeless. When I leave, you may think of such times and wonder — but I must leave. You turn and murmur and today I must tell you that I go as soon as possible, and the house snores and sleeps into the bright Alacay morning and music plays from somewhere and a dog sniffs about and a neighbour borrows a knife and love — this is as far as we come, don't stop me or delay me.

December 21st. You say I want my home — no, not the place where I used to be; returning there will not be to reach home — yes I miss home but it is no longer that one. I'm frightened to leave you behind — no words are correct, there's a huge disorder inside. I'm not of this place, I come from where I learned my disorder (inbred, is it?) and I just don't know, I don't know — but you've been a good man to me, a good friend, the best.

December 22nd. I come home and feel sudden contrition. I'm trying your patience a lot, and know I'm doing it but I don't stop, and I do it because I feel so bad about leaving, and next week I will. I give love with one hand and take it away with the other. You stay patient.

I come in and I whistle for you and suddenly I catch sight of our bed and I begin to make some supper. I prepare the fish for you the way you have shown me. I think of your woman in Dumaguete and pray that I'm not treating you even more badly than I'm already aware, and wonder again at my throwing away what I wanted when it feels so good to have it. My life is waiting for the bus as I did tonight, running across to jump on, looking at the world flash by — I am not happier, but with my self, or nearer by a fraction. I'm happier lying with you and you rub my stomach to chase away the ache, and every small kindness and sacrifice I notice, I love, feel helpless because I can't, I just can't.

Supper is nearly done. I know you'll come back late, and drunk, and won't be hungry, and somehow it makes me more contrite; because of your failings I see my own all too clearly and between 'falls', you keep yourself straight and even, which is more than I do. Funny I should call them 'falls' and you call them 'highs'.

Christmas Day. Wake up to Christmas like any Asian day, and beside my man. Breakfast, back to bed. Up to the Legaspi store for half a gallon of tuba and now we cook and I look across every minute and proud to be with this man and this crazy Christmas and the future just doesn't happen. Outside, the banana trees move ragged as always and the boys pump water and you turn over and I sink back into it, in amongst it all. I don't believe that I'll actually be without you — it must be some sort of joke. I look at your hands and I love them so much. We don't talk about it.

Perhaps the only way to keep away from the edge of things is to live in constant change — is that why I'm doing this? How great my fear, you don't know, you think I want to be home and I let you think it. I can't even show the doubts I have, how can I say: let's stay together one way or another, I want to! But it seems more cruel now than just to go, as if I'm sure of what I'm doing. But I'm not.

Seventeen

8/1/78

Mahal kong Ilong,

How are you love? I felt the tightness in the chest thinking of the idea I might not hear from you again. I am very buang about you, Ilong.

Siloy and family arrived back and happy of the idea that somebody is finally with me at the house. I was afraid that I would be crazy of being here alone any longer and nothing to do. After all the eating and drinking I went for a walk and because it was a full moon and you were with me, I mean assuming you were with me it was a very nice walk. And after that nice walk I feel the tightness in my chest again, thinking that I might lost you. I must not think this way.

There's a delay on my getting a work. Please take a care of yourself.

Rafael.

18/1/78

I just came back from Angeles City and found that it's much harder to get a job there so I just have to wait here in Alacay. I stay with a friend for one meal only and go to the next for another. I start thinking of you again, not that I don't like it. I miss you very much. I can't help thinking that the words I wrote on this letter is not enough.

I'm now on a bus going to Cubao post office. I've got to finish this letter now the post office is opened already. I hoped that your stomach is okay now. Gihigugma ko ikaw.

Rafael.

21/1/78

Mahal kong Ilong,

It is hard for me also to express what I think or how I feel. Sometimes we are so strong and the next moment we are weak, maybe it is because that we think so much that all crazy ideas came into our mind. That at times our life is meaningless. Your letter really brightened my day, it inject life into my weak mind. And I am strong again.

Yes I agree with you about having love and lose it, than not to love at all. It was just those depressed moments when I think otherwise. That will not happen again. I will gamble again with you when you come back.

Yesterday I went beach with my cousin (you never met him) to gather some sea shells. Funny, at the beach I suddenly didn't like to get shells instead I swim, and swim like I never swim before, wow how refreshing to swim, good mentally and physically. I swim for you, I swim for your mother, I swim for everybody – buang na pod no? I will go back again there, I don't know when, since, we work on Sunday also. It was not Cavite but Zapote, about halfway from Alacay to Cavite.

My hair is short now cause I had it shave bare. I still have moustache and of course my pimples still here on my face. But me, I cannot forget your face, it is still vivid to me, maybe because I kiss every part of your face many times no?

I just came from a three hours overtime. I was alone cause the other boys didn't work tonight. That's all now. Please take care and hold on, ha. Ilong I love you. Your love,

Rafael.

7/2/78

Dear Mrs Clarke,

I don't know where to start or how to begin this letter, or this note as I would like to call it so but I've got to do it and, I might say where is Emma. I've wondered if she arrived there or not since it's the 7th February and she left Manila last 28/12/77 and by the way I only heard of her once from Thailand on the second week of Jan.

Hi Ilong – this is part of my unfinished letter for your mother asking for your whereabouts. I was so worried about you. I thought you were lost somewhere or you just don't want to write to me anymore. Today is my lucky day, since it's my first day at work and after work at exactly 5.30 in the afternoon I received your letter. Wow my spirit is surging up again. In the past six weeks I was so down that I don't know what to do and I can't think straight, 'Karon ni balik na ako sa kalibutan.'

I'm very happy that you enjoyed so much your trip. By the way how's your stomach. Is this the reason why you were delayed in writing. Please this is not a reproach or blaming you, I'm just saying this cause I have nothing to say, and I know you have the habit of writing all the time.

Well I'm working now and its hard work but I enjoyed it. That's all for now. I love you.

Rafael.

6/5/78

Hinandum kong Ilong,

Kumusta ka akong Ilong, na hinangop kaayo akong nagbasa sa imong mga sulat, samot na siguro ang imong gibat, human so imong taud-taud nga pag-biyahi.

Nadawat nako ang imong 'postcard' niadtong 18 sa Abril. Usa ka adlaw human sa akong aklaw nga na-tauhan. Dako kayo ang akong kalipay nga gibati, dili ma-tukib.

At the moment I am working at San Juan. It is very hot

at my work, that why my skin colour turn very dark. But it's all right, you have given me an inspiration and hope. Every time I finish work I read your letter. I drink and smoke a bit, it helps as well, after working hard.

If there's anything you wanted to say please, don't hesitate to say it. I can take anything coming from you.

I guess I'm glad that it did not materialise, not that I don't want it, God knows how much I want you to have my child but I've got to be around, be near you at least, someday, somehow.

The heat here is unbearable. I don't know which one is better, your extreme cold there or our extreme heat here. It haven't rain yet since you left.

There's nothing wrong with your writing, how about mine? That's all now. Nagmahal kanunay.

Rafael.

25/5/78

My dear Ilong,

Love, I lost your dark glasses because of my stupidity and I'm very sorry about it. Just when I need it most during my work.

I'm trying to save money for my passport or if I can't save that much then I would borrow some from our company. If I have to pay for the travel tax then it means goodbye for my passport. I might just use the money for the operation of my eye.

We have our first rain and I was working in the rain the whole day. I know you would be excited if you were here. I'm now assigned to work near the Commission of Immigration remember the place? We goes to work at 8.00 am and go off at 5.00 pm. I do the marketing and cooking and the other guys do the cleaning. That's a working man in action.

Have you my last Visayan-English letter, if so tell me about your reaction. I was planning to write all in Visayan but I recall that you didn't have Visayan-English dictionary. Tell me if there's anything you did not understand.

By next week I will be send back to San Juan. I hope I will be send back to Alacay, I can't hardly stand Manila.

Kanusa kaha kita magkita pag-usab no? Naghandum kanimo kanunay.

Rafael.

18/8/78

Mahal kong Ilong,

Cheer up, let's not be too sentimental (look who's talking). If we do we're bound to lost each other. The idea is to get busy or occupied all the time. Remember the night you cried and I didn't, I nearly did. Well I cried a thousand times when you left, entertaining the idea that I would not see you again, now my tears will not fall, maybe I've shed all my tears a long time ago whatever that mean. I, too, are a very sentimental person, it's just the hard work, that I won't have time to be so. And I think, your letters help a lot from my going to pieces or get drunk all the time. By the way, this week I've drunk six bottles of beer only and the week before I had five and no hard liquor for a month now. I drink with the guys at the weekend or we go to the beach at Cavite. That beach has given a nostalgic feeling.

I'm very busy this days and the following weeks. In fact I'm so tired that I go to bed after eating my supper.

I'm sorry about that Visayan-English letter, cause I was thinking you still have that dictionary and you were eager to learn. What a big frustration to you had I stick to my plan of writing all in Visayan.

San Juan is halfway between Manila and Cubao. Remember the first time we walked from Rizal Park to Cubao, a little past of San Juan we rested for a while, nahinumdum ka?

And you've learned my habit of saying no after a sentence, no? Take care. Sa imo nagmahal,

Rafael.

25/8/78

Dear Ilong,

Today I received you letter and feel sad that you are lonely or disturbed about us, and glad also, very glad that you feel the way I do, happy that it's us, we together will journey through our lifespan for a while or all the way, but who knows? Of course I want you back very badly, in fact I want you here now. I don't care of going to other places without you. Any place will be all right for me as long as your around. I don't believe on lottery but I'm going to buy a sweepstake ticket hoping to win to help you for your fare. There's little I can do to help you. I hate to say this but its got to be your move for us to be together. Please tell me what to do to help you. I wish there's something I can do except writing on time. I don't think it was selfishness when you left, in the first place your purpose was to travel to see places and secondly you have to be sure of your feeling. Had you stayed maybe we will be hating each other now. That was the only way to do. But if you think that it's difficult for us to be together then so be it. Tell me now and we can be practical. We can be together through letters only even for life. We don't have to destroy our life if its impossible to be together.

Did you know that you are the only person that I have written so many letters. I don't write to my parents, friends, sweethearts before, for I'm lazy and lack words. If the worst come then I have to move. All my life I've been looking for a home and a city is not my idea of a home.

Let's sing to the love that we both found
even for a day or one year round.

If this is a poem tell me what's wrong with it. I know there's something wrong with it, I just can't put a finger to it.

Our experienced together has changed me a lot. I begin to appreciate nature more. I draw a lot now in fact I have a drawing I want you to see and keep it for me. Will you keep it for me? I'm practising the headstand now.

A love as strong as ours will never lose. All we got to do is keep our patience. Please hold on for a while. To keep you busy please send a drawing of your room or anything you like to draw, like you use to draw. I mean anything.

Don't be sad, remember I felt what you feel when you left. I almost panic by drinking all the time but now we have to get hold of ourselves for us to win. Our love will set us free from this predicament.

I have to go now for I ran out of words again and please don't think of me only, think of yourself. Take care.

Rafael.

25/9/78

Mahal kong Ilong,

Hi love, it's so good to hear that you are working now, very glad. What happened to you happened to me after you left. I have all the time in the world and yet I can't think of anything to do expect lick my bleeding heart and get drunk. But all that is in the past now, we have to think of the present to be able to face the future with high spirit.

I think I have learned a lot from our being together and after you left. Yes I am happy with my work now. I almost love my work which is heavy work and in the open.

We dwell so much on the past and that's why we are so receptive to it because we are very sentimental persons.

If its possible for you to come back we don't have to go out of the Philippines any more. Because it will cost you a lot of money. As long as we can be together that's all that matters now, that is if you like, anywhere. Not that I don't like to go out. I still like to travel. But that's almost impossible for me.

Please understand if my letter is not on time, I know you needed it. I'm trying so hard. You know it takes me three to five days to composed a letter. I'm kind of slow in writing of everything. And we are very busy nowadays. We work on Sunday and work two to three hours every night, and when I'm tired I cannot concentrate. But I do think of you most of the time. I'm not kidding. I really miss you, really.

Oi! I cannot perfect yet the headstand but I keep on trying. Try sleeping outside if it's not very cold, or lie down on the grass for an hour or two (of course, on a starry night). You'll see the beauty of the heavenly bodies. I've done it twice already. Please take care,

Rafael.

26/9/78

Mahal kong Ilong,

I just mailed my last letter when I received your letter this afternoon, and I'm very glad that you've found yourself again if that is the right term.

No, it's not hot anymore but it's wet, it's one storm after another this past two months. I enjoy the rain but there's no work. Most of the places in Manila are flooded and the traffic is terrible.

There are many things that I notice that I didn't before, like the butterfly, or maybe I'm just fascinated by their colour. Wow, what a teacher 'ikaw'.

I just heard that storm signal No 3 has been hoisted here in Luzon. I don't think I can mail this letter today or tomorrow. Everything are suspended today.

I have the same problem with my smoking. The most that I can stay off from smoking is a week. I don't usually smoke when I'm working because it makes me feel drowsy. We will have to try harder.

I don't have a chance yet to move cause I have to pay money I owe from my parents, it will be about a year before I can move. Anyway the place where I am now is okay, it's by the hill and few sari-sari store (you know what I mean), it's far from the main road which is much better.

Nakasabut ako kaayo sa imong sulat ug sa imong balak. You have a very good memory, no?

A year is a long time. Yes, it's a long time not to see or feel the one I love, but since there's nothing we can do we'll have to hold on for a while. We'll have to think that after that one year we may have a lifetime to share (I hope).

See, it took me a week to finish the letter. Love,
Rafael.

22/10/78

Mahal kong Ilong,

Now, its Sunday and I am here in Cavite with my fore-
man from work who love to swim also. The water is low, I
mean the tide is very low and oily. I swim for a while back
and forth. There's so many people cause it's Sunday. I watch
people swim and others on the beach. My memory is in
the time when we were here, now I am living in the past
again. I could see the sand castle you built but I could not
tear my eyes from you. Why did I have to meet you and lost
you. I am a very pessimistic person, I can't help it. I am a
very buang person. Sometimes I wonder what you see in
me, or why you like me. You're probably buang too.

I wonder if you received my letter. I've send three letters
after your last letter, or maybe you were just very busy. Sa
imo naghulat,

Rafael.

16/11/78

My dear Ilong,

I've been trying to get a sleep for hours and I cannot
sleep. So I finally stand and write this letter. It seems I'm
impatient or restless again. I can't understand myself again.
I have to calm down in thinking. Maybe I'm not tired
enough to sleep, I must work hard some more to be so
tired, so that my mind would not wander in the past and
the future. It seem that your the only person that I can

talk to. (Buang gyud ako.) I hate to admit it, but, it seem I depend so much on your letter for strength. I read your letters again and again. I have to be patient. (Patient, patient.) Enough of buang-buang.

To quote your words, it is a cry of pleasure to received a letter from you, specially the last one when I'm so down. And I am very lucky too, much too lucky (I hope my luck will hold on).

Yes, I love to go out from here also, if it's possible. I really been wanting to go out for a long time. And, also it would be selfish of me to ask you to stay here with me. If your mind is not with me we will not be happy here. Sige, if it's possible to be with you and be near your mother, okay na lang. The point is, I can be with you, I think that is all that matter, even anywhere. And I promise to wait for you and be patient.

Yes, it's amazing how we are staying together this long. I was even pessimistic at first but now I'm not anymore. I'm happy again. Sige na ha! I'm sleepy already. Sorry about the paper, I have no other to hand. With love,

Rafael.

23/11/78

Mahal kong Ilong,

It's 9 pm. Already, and I have just got off from three hours overtime. I happened to glance at your last letter while I was putting the mosquito net in its proper place, and I thought that I would write a few lines for you.

Yes there was one storm after another here but it was just heavy rain here in Manila. The strong wind were in the northern part of Luzon (thus facing the China Sea).

The other night I sleep or rather I lie down in open and watch the moon and the stars. It was on a pile of lumber that I lie down. It is very refreshing. I have a nice head afterward and can sleep right away. I stayed there for a few hours only cause the wind subside and my mortal enemy mosquito keep on biting me.

Yes the feeling is mutual. I really wish that you are here now with me. Sus, pastilan pag-kamingaw kaayo da. Let's hear from you on the next mail. Your love,

Rafael.

14/12/78

Mahal kong Ilong,

It's December now and I'm more than a year now here in Manila, and it's almost a year now when you left. Time passes so quickly no? I wish I could put it more in words of what I feel, but I lack it.

I am here now with Siloy talking about work and talking about you also of course over a local whisky in a Remy Martin bottle.

I have to cut this letter short now cause I have a long way to walk for San Jose suburb where I stay. Your love,

Rafael.

20/12/78

Mahal kong Ilong,

I'm doing fine here, thank you. Ikaw kumusta ka? I do hope that you're fine also. Maybe, I would freeze to death there, no?

You are spoiling me, which I'm glad of it. I think we both needed it. I hope we keep on spoiling each other.

I think I understand your feeling, it's maybe your staying in a big city which I feel the same. If you do come back don't worry about your bringing sadness to me. With joy or sadness just come, and we'll worry about that later. Maybe when I go there I will feel the same, or maybe not. I don't worry about things any more except how to give my love. You must teach me how.

With you maybe I can live in the country with something to do like farming or fishing. In London it would be part of the time, I won't survive there longer.

I finished this letter in Tio Ramon's house. I talk to Tio Ramon for a while over two bottles of San Miguel and the sound of 'Nocturne in B Flat Major,' by Roger Williams.

Your own,

Rafael.

8/1/79

Mahal kong Ilong,

Petra (the cat) and me watching the grasshopper about to take off, upon seeing that Petra wasn't interested in him, the hopper relaxes. My eyes followed Petra's walk to the pavement, wow! What a grace a cat have. When I look at the hopper again he was gone.

I spend the 24th and 25th of Christmas with Tio Ramon and I think I made a right decision in my choice of a place on a time like that. We talked about music and travel down nostalgia road for a while then he goes to bed. I made my bed downstairs of course (you know where) and start with my occupation on my free time, thinking of you. To me thinking of you is like touching the cat, watching the moon and the stars on the top of the lumber pile, the insects and the butterfly on my daily stroll, the butterfly most specially. I hope that my fascination with butterfly never stop. I'm buang again, no?

Sus! Buang kaayo, no? Where were we, ah! On eve of New Year I was back with Tio Ramon with Siloy, we spend two nights there and go back to Alacay early in the morning of the 2nd to work.

Anyway, I give plenty of warm air inside this envelope to keep you warm. I read it on the papers that there's a blizzard and it's very cold in the whole of Europe. You must be staying indoors most of the time, no? I wish I were with you now to share that coldness. Gugma,

Rafael.

18/1/79

Mahal kong Ilong,

Honey you are not mad, I'm sure of it, otherwise you'll not be writing to me like that. You've travelled to Asia and you've seen the pace of life here which is very little pressure and that's the kind of life you like (me too), naturally you will feel the pressure of the city.

Ilong, you have time to come back now? Dali dayon, sus, kadugay ba, makulba ab man ta nimo, please don't get buang kaayo, cause I might get buang also kaayo. Can I have the pleasure of your company to get buang kaayo with me, no? Now we can watch the butterflies together, a child's first glimpse of the world – butterflies and branches and water and fish and life and earth and tears and joy... can we do it together, can you teach me to improve my English?

This is the early part of the morning of the 19th at Muntinlupa post office, I'm trying to finish this letter under a tree, and the flowers inside the envelope is from that tree, and the petals landed on my head. Please, get out from that hole you are in. I feel sad that I cannot do something, I haven't changed, I have learned many things a lot of things from you, my meat-eating time have been lessen a great deal, and I feel proud of it, but I'm asking my mouth to co-operate.

We have so many things to do together that we won't have time for boredom. That's all na, ha? So I can mail this right away, no? Your loving,

Rafael.

2/2/79

Mahal kong Ilong,

Up to now I still love you and I hope that it stays that way. You see, for example even that I don't love you I would still miss you, I mean really miss you. But, I love you, that means my longing is more. I don't know how to say everything. But then if I know how to write everything in one sitting then we won't be writing most often (I don't like that). You didn't know then, that you can come back anytime you want. If you want to come back or feel very buang there, you should have right away. I appreciated very much your respecting my plans but if you get very buang then I get very annoyed with myself. Please believe me that I would get very buang here also. Please come na, or get out of London. Gusto ko ikaw ang akong Valintina,

Rafael

26/2/79

Mahal kong Ilong,

At last I finally heard from you, I was a little bit worried of you. I thought you were very buang already. I'm glad you are happy and alive again. I send you two letters, didn't you received them, then there's something wrong with the mail (who's mail?).

I meet up with Charles and Valerie yesterday evening who are in Manila. We had our supper together, Charles was cooking (he can cook now) and everybody was talking, talk coming England down to Singapore then swing to Alacay then linger for a while in Dumaguete where everybody stayed for a while in the past. I talk to Charles while he was cooking, I had the urge to join him in cooking but then I have learned from the past not to interfere. After a while, after a long while I felt that emptiness again, you were a part of the scene and I was sad and felt the pang of loneliness for I was the only one who can see you, I was just wondering what did you leave in me that I long so much for you.

My reason and plan is this. For a while the money I owe my family was a problem to me. I thought I would pay first the money I owe them before I go anyplace I like, but when I told mother about it she just said to have my eye operated through the money I owe them, and I can pay them later when I'm not very tied up (I don't know when). So I can do or we can do what we want now, since your tired of London. My plan is this, for us to go together to Palawan, since both of us haven't gone there yet. I think that's the best place for us to start, the soil is rich and both of us can survive through farming (I think). But I wonder if I could catch fish again. I still eat fish but I don't know if I will spear a fish again. Remember when we saw those fish in Cubao, I said the fish are beautiful no? and you said why do you kill them. That started me to thinking to live and let live. But I don't have the strength to stop it abruptly, but I think I'm coming along.

It's hard for me to communicate properly, please don't

get me wrong, I want you now here, I'm tired of here and now. There's too many people. I'm planning to go by end of April or first week of May. That is, if it is possible with you.

I'm schedule to be operated on Friday the 9th of March. Please take care. Your love,

Rafael.

15/3/79

Mahal kong Ilong,

I'm writing this letter now at the hospital while waiting for my turn to be operated. There's quite a long line, I'm number 36.

I received your letter yesterday morning and I could not help to feel the emptiness inside upon learning that your not coming yet, I'm very impatient, no? I have to control myself, I have to be patient. It should be enough that you write, I would not ask so much from you, sige lang, I'll have to wait.

Wow, I'm nervous like a kid on his way to the dentist. I hope they'll call me now and get over with it, cause I got cold feet.

16th March, after the operation it was a bad day, I hope this won't happened again.

17th March. It's an effort but I want to finish this letter, sige lang, take your time and be happy and please take care of yourself, ha? I'm on sick leave now up to the 25th of this month and I don't know what to do. That's all for now

Love

Rafael

Eighteen

May '98

Dear Emma,

Kumusta ka? You letter came as a very pleasant surprised. I received it before I went to Mindanao for a two weeks visit. I went directly to Oroquieta, remember? And it was fiesta time. Then off to Sibukay. The grand old man Tatay (of the stentorian voice) has been dead the last two years. I showed them all your letter; they are glad that after all these years you have resurrected. The years of silence seem insignificant. Only I have the dilemma of using a second language.

The changes are visible everywhere. In my greying hair and the washed-out beaches, all evince the hand of nature. No, I have not married or have children either. Do you mind that very much, Emma? You write there is a curse on you. But, these things were not for us after all, we do not need to tread this path perhaps. We can espouse ideas.

I am sorry to disappoint, but I have not heard from

Rafael all this time. In '88 I met a guy who told me Rafael was believed to be on a ferry that was sunk. But there is not confirmation and meanwhile no word either. What was your dream Emma? Perhaps the enormous welling of emotions may have penetrated through your dream, I don't know.

The turmoil of our peoples has taken many and returned few. I was dragged into the socio-political quagmire of my beloved islands – my chance for happiness, my dreams of writing, the dream is gone, but I have survived. I still climb mountains.

It is one o'clock in the afternoon. I can see the sky through the rotting nipa roof of my shack. Not in my old hut beside the creek but another portion of the farm. I lost all my books in a fire – my Neruda, Eliot, Wordsworth etc. It wasn't the house I miss, it was those poems. In a place where books are hard to come by it was a tragedy. They were my balm. Perhaps it was what pushed Dylan Thomas to self-destruction, the clash between reality and the imagined world.

Like my country, I have had to retrench. The third world dangles on the hook. Trouble and fighting has erupted several times; the hold of the ruling elites are becoming a bit shaky. The country is modernised by the process of consumerism but without developing it. The sea is no longer as clear as before – too much flotsam.

I am sorry my friend if I run on the mouth, but my learning hasn't been perfect. We had to scrounge around for it and it wasn't always there for the taking. Perhaps that is why the word 'muddied' always appears in my poems, the lament of a third-worlder.

Salutations!

Alphonse.

October '98

Dear Emma,

It is mid-morning and the northeast wind blows coolly from Sumilon island. I opened your gift a few minutes ago, came across Prufrock, and I have to sigh Emma, for sure as sure can be, he sounds at times like me. So Eliot was there too. As if I didn't know. I was surprised to note the package was dated sometime last June. The snail must be on our side of the ocean. Perhaps the world instead is getting bigger.

It's nice to be holding the pen once in a while instead of a glass. Actually I hadn't touch the stuff for almost a week now, no thanks to any sense of moderation on my part but to a really bad bum stomach which reminded me of my mortality. Wasn't it just the day before when we thought we were immortals?

As for me, not a penny to be had. Happy with nothing but the chirping birds. It's easier to live in the forest with your cats and dogs, singing birds for a radio, the blue sky for a TV. Rimbaud at eighteen must have grown tired of the hole in his pockets, threw away his pen, went off to Africa and became a smuggler. So much hot air to fly a balloon. I should have planted camotes instead. But really, I was no cheap two bits either, such a fine mind only gone to seed with drink and dope. But what choice did I have? It was either to the bank looking smart with a tie – I'd rather be mad and poor than sober with a tie; I would not care to be caught dead in one. Ahem.

It is afternoon now and I'm going to the beach in a while. Life moves on and I often times don't know where it goes. I will not say now that I don't give a damn. It will not be honest for deep down I care.

Definitely I am going to mail this letter tomorrow. I am sorry I waxed philosophical my friend.

Salutations!

Alphonse.

Roads Ahead